# PIER PRESSURE

CODY MARLOWE

Published by Central Avenue Press

ISBN (EPUB): 979-8-9943006-0-2

ISBN (Paperback): 979-8-9943006-1-9

# RITUALS OF A RESPECTABLE STREET

The law office on Central looked out over a street that never quite decided whether it was respectable. In daylight you got retirees with the paper under one arm and a bag from the five-and-dime under the other, the breeze off the bay pushing exhaust along like a tired usher. By night, neon claimed the glass—pink on the café, a buzzing blue at the arcade—so the windows caught color the way a church catches afternoon sun.

Robert Kelly unlocked the front door before seven, as he always did, the old brass key turning with the small complaint of a habit. Inside: the smell of floor wax and paper, the hum of the ceiling fans that pretended at summer. He stood a second just to listen—building sigh, fan's soft blade-whisper, a far car rolling a light—and felt himself settle into the morning like a shirt he knew would fit.

He flicked on lamps one by one. The reception desk. Margaret's typewriter. The framed certificate that said KELLY & GREER in respectable letters, though the practice had been more grit than polish since the day they hung the shingle. He set his briefcase down and smoothed the stack he'd left last night: one divorce, one probate, one small criminal thing that shouldn't have been but was.

The ritual steadied him. Ritual was why he kept his shirts in order, why he shaved before dawn with hot water and a careful hand, why he said grace at dinner even when his mind wandered. Ritual let a man pretend the ocean outside the city couldn't surprise him with a sudden storm.

He poured coffee in the back, that tin percolator bubbling like an old friend with a story it told every morning. Out the rear window, the alley waited—dumpsters, a cat that had adopted Margaret, a strip of sky already too bright. He stirred sugar in, watched the swirl, told himself the day would stay inside the edges if he kept it slow.

By seven-thirty he had a pen in his hand and the divorce file open. Mrs. Harper wanted the Buick not because she needed it but because it would mean he wouldn't have it, and that was the point. Robert listened to her every time she came in and wrote down the same sentences as if the repetition could wear the anger to a smooth stone.

The door clicked at eight. Margaret. She moved like someone who understood buildings and the men inside them. Hair set Saturday mornings on 22nd Avenue, glasses low on her nose, a dress the color of a church fan. "Morning, Mr. Kelly," she said, setting her purse down, already peeling the dust cover off the typewriter. She fed paper in with the grace of a nurse hanging a bag.

"Morning, Margaret."

She looked over the top of her glasses at his desk. "You've been here since before the sun had manners."

"Light docket is a myth," he said.

She smiled without committing to it. "Mr. Greer will be

in 'ten minutes' that cost thirty. He called. Said to tell you he's 'flying.'"

"Of course," Robert said, and felt the usual tug at the corner of his mouth.

He could mark time by Tommy Greer. The way the door opened when he came in—fast, a little loud—the flash of a smile that made people forgive the lateness. Plant City still clung to his voice, sunshine baked into syllables. Robert had known him long enough to recognize two versions: the courtroom showman who could make a probate judge lean forward, and the quiet one who leaned too close over a brief and spoke low like confession without a priest.

He pretended to read while he waited, eyes following words he'd already memorized. The street offered its morning—delivery truck idling, a bus hissing to a stop, the café owner rolling out the chalkboard menu. He liked the ordinary. Liked that if you looked down Central from the window, the inverted pyramid of the Pier sat where it always sat, an odd shape at the end of a straight line. A fixed point. A compass, if you needed one.

The door flew at eight forty-two.

"Morning to the honest and the beautiful," Tommy said, because he always opened with something unserious. Tie not quite tight, hair a little longer than prudent, the jacket slung like he'd been born with a shoulder made for it. He crossed the room in those quick strides, the kind that turned a hallway into a stage. He thumped his briefcase on the conference table and grinned with his whole face at Margaret. "You look ten years younger, which brings you to —what, twenty-six?"

Margaret didn't look up. "Save it for the judge, Mr. Greer."

"Won't work on him." Tommy swung to Robert, lowering

the grin into a gentler smile like dropping your voice in a church. "We ready?"

"We're always ready," Robert said, which meant I have done the work, which meant I have already run this in my head twice.

Tommy loosened his tie, then tightened it, a nervous, thoughtless tic that felt younger than the rest of him. He sat on the edge of Robert's desk without asking and looked down at the divorce file as if a quick glance could grant understanding. "She still wants the Buick?"

"She wants him to feel it," Robert said.

Tommy nodded. "Don't we all."

He said it lightly and the room changed anyway. Something tuned itself tighter, barely audible, the way a radio shifts a fraction and a voice comes into focus. Robert didn't look up. He drew a bracket on the page and wrote a date and put his pen on top of it like a lid.

Across the street the café lit its open sign. The neon caught on the window glass and threw a stripe of pink across Tommy's sleeve. Robert watched it out of the corner of his eye and thought—not for the first time—that some colors weren't meant for daylight. They belonged to the hour when the city felt like it might forgive a man if he asked right.

————

Lunch happened at the metal tables on the café sidewalk, because Tommy liked to be where people walked. He said it reminded him the town existed outside of legal pads. They ate while old men clicked dominoes, the sound like small bones. Robert's sandwich left grease on his napkin that drew a dark shape where his fingers rested, and he stared at it too long before folding it away.

"You ever think about quitting?" Tommy asked through the last of an espresso, syrup-sweet and gone too fast.

"Quitting what?"

"The part where we pretend it's all enough. Wills and cars and who keeps the dog." He set the cup down gently, tapped it with a fingertip as if testing whether it might ring. "Sometimes it feels like I'm arguing little storms while the hurricane sits at the edge of the map."

Robert chewed carefully. He looked past Tommy to the street, where a woman with a blue scarf crossed against the light and didn't hurry. "Storms ruin roofs. People need roofs."

Tommy grinned. "You're good at that."

"At what."

"Building reasons that keep you safe." He leaned back in the chair, and the metal made a soft noise like a question. "I'm not saying run. I'm saying—there's a whole bay out there. Could drive till the water looks different."

"The water is the water," Robert said, but even to his own ear it sounded like a prayer said because it was written and not because it was believed.

He didn't look at Tommy then because looking was dangerous. He watched the window instead, where their reflections sat faint on the glass: two men not quite touching, the inverted pyramid small between their heads like an idea no one had the nerve to name.

A breeze off the water lifted the edges of the napkins and the paper cups; one skittered and Robert pinned it quickly with his palm. Tommy laughed. "Quick hands," he said.

"I was Navy once," Robert said. "You learn to hold what's loose."

"You let go of some things too," Tommy said. "Or they take you down."

Margaret would later say that if anyone had bothered to look—really look—they'd have seen it right there on a Thursday with the dominoes clicking: a conversation that never said its true name and still wrote itself on the air between two men. But no one looked. That was one kind of mercy.

————

Rain came in right after lunch, not the big theatrical kind that slapped the bay but the long curtain you barely noticed until your hair was damp and your shirt stuck. Central Street went reflective; lights smeared along the asphalt like someone had dragged a thumb through paint.

The courthouse closed early. Margaret gathered her purse and her good umbrella. "You'll both go home before mildew sets in," she said without looking up from the ribbon she was changing.

"We will," Tommy promised. Robert said nothing. Promises made out loud felt like daring the wrong listener to take notes.

By five it was just the two of them and the hum of the fans, the city outside softened to a blur. Tommy perched on the edge of the window and spun a pen the way some men twirl a coin. "You ever go to the pier at night?" he asked, casual.

Robert's throat went dry for no decent reason. "With my kids. Ice cream. Fireworks sometimes."

"That's not night," Tommy said, and smiled. "That's evening."

Robert looked at him then, because some conversations you can't have with your eyes on paperwork. Tommy's face changed up close—the show peeled back, the muscle under it visible in the jaw, the tired not from work. His tie was loose. There was a smudge on his cuff like he'd leaned the wrong place and hadn't noticed.

"Don't," Robert said, and wasn't sure which direction he meant: don't finish the sentence, don't invite me, don't make it real.

Tommy nodded like he'd heard all three. He set the pen on the windowsill and watched it roll until it knocked gently against the frame and stopped. "I'll go alone then," he said lightly, and the lightness was the worst part. "Check whether the jukebox at Hank's still works on the first try."

Robert looked at the pen. At the stripe of café neon now more electric against rain, as if the water fed the color. "You don't have to announce where you're going," he said.

"Who am I announcing to?" Tommy shrugged, then let his voice fall. "Maybe to myself."

They let silence fill the room because talking any more would have meant telling the truth, and the building wasn't made for that kind of weather. The clock on the wall made a sound like a drip in a sink, patient. Robert put papers into his briefcase very carefully, each stack neat, corners true. He told himself he was a man who cleaned up before he left a room.

At the door he said, "You'll catch cold in that shirt."

Tommy grinned. "I'll let it."

Robert nodded and stepped into the hall. The stairwell smelled like wood that had seen a hundred summers. He took the stairs by habit and counted them without meaning to. On the landing he stopped, hand on the banister, because some part of him had expected to be called back. He waited three slow breaths, like listening for a verdict in a room you're not allowed to enter, then went down into the soft rain.

Outside, the café chairs stood on their tables like tired

dancers. A kid on a bike cut a tight circle in the wet and grinned at no one. Robert walked to his car and sat a moment with the engine off, palms on the wheel. The rain made a sound on the hood like a hundred small decisions he didn't remember making.

He started the car and turned, not toward home, not at first. The angle of the street, the habit of his hand, the quiet gravity of a man's weakest wish—all of it drew him east until the road offered him the long line toward the water. The Pier rose at the end, lit strange and stubborn, a geometry that refused apologies.

He didn't stop. He let the sight of it be enough. That was the lie he told himself—enough—while the wipers kept time and the radio played a song he didn't register except that a man was singing about a door he couldn't open and a window he couldn't close.

He went home by a different route, because sometimes a map is a kind of conscience.

———

Crescent Lake wore evening like a pressed shirt. Porch lights came on in a polite wave; sprinklers ticked a soft metronome across small lawns. Elaine had left the light by the kitchen door on, the way she always did when rain promised to make the threshold a place you might hesitate.

"You're late," she said, not angry, towel in her hands, the counters already clean. Flour dusted the edge of the sink. The smell of chicken and rosemary lived in the air the way church incense does if you sit in a pew long after Mass.

"Courthouse closed early," he said, and even as he said it he knew it answered nothing.

She angled her head as if listening past his voice to the room behind it. "Father Donnelly called. The parish wants you to read next Sunday. He says you've a steady voice."

Robert hung his jacket like a man who'd been taught what to do with his hands. "I'll read," he said, and felt the words settle in his mouth like a wafer dissolving.

At dinner the children told the world the way children do: the spelling test, the boy who cried on the playground and then didn't, Sister Agnes's story about saints who bled flowers. Elaine smiled and asked the right questions and cut the chicken into small squares for the small fork. Robert nodded and passed salt and thought— you could live inside this and be righteous and still have a room somewhere in the city that knows your other name.

After dishes, Elaine pressed a shirt into his hands, warm from the iron. "Saturday is the fundraiser," she said, more reminder than warning. "The Bishop might attend."

"I'll be there."

She reached to adjust his collar as if he were a picture she could level. Up close she smelled like Ivory soap and starch, like the house itself. "You're pale," she said.

"Rain," he said.

She studied him one heartbeat longer than comfortable, then let him go. "Say your prayers," she said, not sharp, not soft. Instruction.

They knelt at the bed and he said the words he'd been taught to say, and his voice sounded steady enough that a man who didn't know him would think he was a certain kind of good. Elaine's beads clicked through her fingers; she could pray a rosary as if counting weren't counting at all but music.

Robert closed his eyes and tried to imagine the ocean as a blank thing, not the mirror it had become. He pictured the inverted pyramid at night, hovering like a question someone else had written on the horizon. In the dark of his head he stood on the boards and didn't turn when footsteps came. He woke before the ending.

———

Morning brought sun like it had been forgiven for something. The rain had washed the air without managing to cool it. Robert's alarm rattled at five-thirty and he swung his legs out of bed with the motion of a man who trusts muscle memory more than thought. In the mirror the silver at his temples showed a little more; he combed it back and told himself that was dignity.

Elaine moved in the kitchen with the quiet efficiency of a woman who'd memorize a recipe and then give it away without writing it down. The children ate cereal and spoke with their mouths full because the day was too big to wait. "You'll be at the fundraiser?" she said again as he kissed her cheek. She didn't have to ask. Asking had always been another ritual.

"Of course," he said.

On 4th Street the sun threw long lines. The inverted pyramid sat ridiculous and beautiful, and he looked at it as he always did, like men glance at a clock they already know the time on. At the office Margaret had beaten him for once; she looked up from the typewriter and smiled a smile that meant I know when you're early and when you're merely on time.

"Morning," she said, and slid a stack across. "The will. The divorce. The boy who borrowed a car that didn't belong to him."

Robert took the stack and felt the weight. Paper lies about heft; ink does not.

Tommy arrived late and beaming, like the sun had a favorite. He clapped Robert on the shoulder with a warmth that might have been too much if Robert had not already braced for it. "Jenkins probate at ten," Tommy said. "I'm going to sing the widow a song about the dignity of small things."

"You could just cite the code," Robert said.

"Words move, Rob. Law only works if you get a body to shift an inch." He leaned closer, lowering his voice to that not-for-Margaret register. "Come out tonight."

"Where."

Tommy's smile tilted. "You know where."

Robert put his pen down and picked it up again. "No."

"Okay," Tommy said, and meant not okay at all. He stepped back and the room lost a degree of heat.

By noon they'd won a small thing and talked a bigger thing to a draw. The café sent coffee through the air, sweet strong stuff that made men think they could be more awake than they were. The city settled into its afternoon—humid, a little lazy, pretending the water didn't have moods.

Robert watched the street and told himself the day was a page you could turn without tearing. He wrote a note in the margin of Mrs. Harper's file—BUICK NOT A VEHICLE, A VERDICT—and underlined it and smiled at himself for the indulgence. He thought of the pier and the door Tommy hadn't said and the motel lane farther south where neon tried to be discreet and failed.

He told himself a sentence that had carried him from nineteen to this desk: A man's choices are fences he builds to keep himself from running into the water. He believed it most of the time. He believed it now until Tommy laughed at something Margaret said and the sound came across the room and undid a piece of the fence with a small, neat pry.

Robert capped his pen. "Let's work," he said, and they

did, and the day went forward the way they all do, which is to say it walked itself to the edge of night and didn't look down.

## 2

## WEATHER TALK

The city woke with the stubborn cheer of a place that had decided weather was a rumor. By nine, the streets had a shine at the edges where last night's rain still clung in seams and curb dips, and the bay threw light at the buildings like a cat flicking water from its paw.

Robert arrived a few minutes later than he meant to and earlier than anyone would notice. Margaret's typewriter already clicked, a clean steady metronome that made paperwork feel like music if you didn't listen too hard.

"Morning," she said, sliding a pink message slip across the desk with two fingers. "Mrs. Harper. Twice. I told her the Buick can't answer the phone."

"Thank you." He tucked the slips under a file like you tuck a thought behind a better one.

He loosened his shoulders, opened the probate folder, and tried to let routine take the wheel. He wrote a note in his margin—WITNESS ORDER—then re-wrote it because his hand had thought ahead of him. The hall offered noise: a laugh from someone downstairs, the soft clack of a shoe with a loose heel, the murmur that said the café had filled. He didn't look at the window.

Tommy came in with a wind to him that didn't match the still heat. He paused in the doorway, eyes adjusting to office light, and for a half-breath Robert thought he'd turn and leave like a man who'd opened the wrong room. Then Tommy caught himself, smiled the practiced smile that worked on juries and women who liked charming trouble, and swung inside.

"Saint Margaret," he said, "you sound like a newsroom."

"That will be the headline," she said. "'Men at Work. Film at eleven.'"

Tommy grinned, then found Robert with his eyes the way a man finds the horizon at sea to remember which direction is real. The grin eased. He tapped knuckles twice on Robert's doorjamb and leaned in. "Jenkins. You found me a case note I can pretend I remembered?"

Robert slid the file over. Their fingers didn't touch. Tommy's jacket smelled faintly of wool warmed in a car and the unbranded aftershave men bought at drugstores because they understood the names. The smell reached and was gone, the way a memory tries the handle and lets go.

"Witness order," Robert said.

"Of course," Tommy said, as if the idea had always been in his pocket. He didn't sit. He watched the street over Robert's shoulder. "You sleep?" he asked, voice pitched too casually to be casual.

"Enough."

"Me too," Tommy lied.

They made a shape of the morning out of motions they knew. Phone, file, note, nod. Margaret's keys kept time. A courier dropped something and left peppermints from his pocket on the desk as if payment were a joke everyone enjoyed. The fan over Robert's head squeaked once at the same spot in its spin.

At ten-thirty, a woman named Caldwell arrived to sign something her husband had asked for in a tone that made it sound like a blessing. She smelled faintly of Vick's and laundry. Robert explained the words and she nodded, her pen hovering as if she could hear the paper breathing. "I trust you," she said, and the sentence pressed a thumb on his chest.

After she left, Tommy closed Robert's door halfway—not quite privacy, not quite performance. He stood with his shoulder against the frame, the posture of men who talk to themselves when they're alone. "I went to the pier," he said, eyes on the carpet.

Robert kept his pen on the page. "I thought you might."

"The water was black and loud and the gulls looked like bad ideas. I stood until my shirt stuck to me. There were sailors. A couple that didn't know they were talking too loud. Two kids with a radio that made the same song a hundred times."

Robert wrote a date he didn't need. "Then you went home."

Tommy smiled without teeth. "Sure."

The pen paused. "Don't."

"To what?" Tommy asked. He pushed off the jamb and let the door swing open again, as if the room needed air. "There's a jukebox on 4th that sometimes works on the first try," he said, like a man reciting a weather report. "I didn't go in."

Robert set the pen down. "We're at work," he said.

"I know," Tommy said, and left it there like a book with a finger in the page.

———

Lunch became a walk because sitting felt like confession. They took Central toward the bay, humidity sitting low to the ground like fog that had lost its dignity. The cigar shop door chimed as they passed, and a man at the counter said something in Spanish that made the owner laugh with relief.

"Father Donnelly called my house," Robert said, and heard how quickly the words had come. "Wants me to read Sunday."

"You have a good voice," Tommy said. "Like a radio no one argues with."

"It feels like lying when I'm tired," Robert said, and immediately wished he hadn't.

Tommy didn't look at him. "Maybe you're telling the truth louder than you meant to."

They reached the end of the street where the water begins. The inverted pyramid sat in the heat like a dare and a joke pinned together. A boy threw bread at gulls and flinched when they came close, thrilled and frightened in the same breath.

"Plant City never had water like this," Tommy said. "Everything there ended at a grove, not a horizon. You could pretend the world was rows."

"And now?"

"Now it's edges." He glanced at Robert and away. "You can fall off an edge."

"You can also turn around," Robert said.

Tommy laughed once. "Or jump and call it flying until the ground makes its argument."

Robert watched a sailboat cut the bay like a letter opener that never found a letter. He imagined a life unlabeled: no lector, no partner, no husband, no father. The thought arrived like a thief—efficient, uninterested in your protests—and stood very still until he saw it. He folded it into his pocket like contraband and turned back toward work.

They didn't touch on the walk back. They didn't speak much either. What they did—matching pace, adjusting stride to the other—was its own grammar. Margaret looked up when they came in, eyes tracking them like a metronome finds a beat. She returned to her keys and added carbon paper as if the day required copies.

———

Late afternoon brought a divorce consult that turned into a story about a dog, which was really a story about a marriage. Robert listened, the way he did when listening was the only useful work. The woman talked until the anger wore thin and the ache showed underneath. He wrote the facts carefully and left the rest on the surface of the desk where only he could see it.

Tommy handled a phone call with a judge who didn't believe in extensions, and he kept his voice respectful in the particular way lawyers do when they intend to press anyway. He hung up and leaned his forehead against the cool glass for a second like a man who remembered something too late.

At five-fifteen Margaret stood, smoothed her dress, and put the dust cover on the typewriter like a ritual you say so night will truly begin. "Go home," she told them both, soft. "This city makes a meal of people who think they work better in the dark."

Tommy saluted her. "Yes, ma'am."

She paused at the door, pushed her glasses up with one knuckle, and looked between them as if there were a question posted on the air she could grade. "Careful," she said, and left.

The office grew a different kind of quiet when she was gone. The fan found its squeak again. The street's sound shifted from errands to evening. Tommy sat on the edge of the conference table, palms flat against wood, and looked at the closed door like it was heavy.

"Your wife will be organizing the fundraiser now," he said.

"Yes."

"She's good at that. Being in charge without making it a show."

"She is," Robert said, and felt every correct thing in the sentence cut against him anyway.

Tommy lifted one hand from the table and let it hover in the stale air between them, palm tipped like a man about to swear. He set it back. "Say the word," he said, very quiet, "and we will not be the kind of men who talk around the important thing until it's the only thing left in the room."

Robert swallowed. "And then what kind of men would we be."

"The kind who tell the truth before it tells on us."

Robert looked at the blinds. At the dust caught in the slats—each line of it lit by the late sun like script in a language God understood and people pretended to. "We are at work," he said again, because it was the fence he still believed might hold.

Tommy nodded. "Tomorrow then," he said. It wasn't a question.

––––––

Evening at the Kelly house unfolded in proper order, which is not the same as peace. Elaine folded hymnals into a tote with the neat hands of a woman counting grace. Matthew showed his father a plastic model airplane wing that refused to stay stuck; Robert held it while the glue set and told a story about an aircraft carrier that didn't make him sound young. Anna practiced her spelling and asked what "faithful" meant. Elaine answered first.

After bedtime, Elaine waited at the sink with her fingers pressed on the rim like a woman steadying a boat that rocks more than she likes. "You're thinner," she said.

"I'm not," he said.

"You're not here," she said, and the sentence landed softer than a slap and worse.

He dried his hands. "The practice—"

"Don't use the practice to talk around me," she said, kind and merciless. "I know what work looks like. I also know what a man looks like when he is about to stop being the man he promised to be."

He felt the floor tip under him, just enough to make the cupboard door touch his hip. "I'm here."

"For now," she said, and left him with the clean kitchen and the tick of the clock that made the room sound more empty than quiet.

He tried to pray in bed. The words came. The meaning lagged behind like a child keeping up because it knows it should, not because it wants to see where you're going. Beside him, Elaine's breathing steadied slow and even the way good sleep does, and he lay there listening until the rhythm felt like a thing he might not be invited to anymore.

Sometime after midnight, rain found the roof again. Not loud. Just enough that you knew the bay had rolled over, that the city turned its face on the pillow and asked for another hour.

Robert stared at the ceiling and told himself the morning would make the world simpler.

## 3

# THE FUNDRAISER

The parish hall had been polished into a kind of brightness that made people stand up straighter. Folding chairs in regimented rows, rented linens the color of seashells, raffle baskets bowed within an inch of their lives. A banner stenciled in tidy letters read ST. JUDE'S FALL FUNDRAISER, and beneath it the air held a mix of coffee, floor wax, and perfume that tried to sound like money.

Elaine lived in the center of it, clipboard in hand, moving through the tasks like a waltz she could dance even if the music stopped. She checked the cash box, aligned the hymnals on the choir table, thanked a woman for two pies and redirected a man who wanted to reorganize what did not need reorganizing. When she caught Robert's eye across the room, she gave him the quick small smile she reserved for public agreement—Thank you for being here; please don't make me worry.

He stood near the raffle display and rehearsed steadiness. The second reading he would deliver on Sunday sat in his pocket like a smooth stone. He could feel the verse even now, the cadence fitting his mouth as surely as any argument he'd ever made in court. Love is patient. He took a breath that did not feel patient at all.

"Robert," said Mrs. Genaro from the altar guild, squeezing his hand in both of hers. "You'll read for us? I told Father—your voice is like the old radios. The kind men trust."

"So I've been told," he said, and smiled as if the compliment were an old coat he liked.

Behind him, volunteers fussed over a quilt someone had donated, the pattern a busy geometry of tiny squares that made your eyes work for it. "It's hand-pieced," a woman said to her friend, reverent. "Months and months." Robert thought of the invisible hours in it—needles and lamplight, coffee going cool while someone stitched the same line until the piece obeyed.

The Bishop had sent regrets. The monsignor came instead with a smooth laugh and the comfortable paunch of a man whose dinners were never rushed. He shook Robert's hand and praised the parish and made a joke about raffle tickets that landed halfway and still earned the necessary sound. Fathers, mothers, children circled the tables with paper cups of punch that looked like medicine and tasted like sugar. The air hummed with the safe topics—school, weather, the team, the new family who'd joined and would be in the eight o'clock pew.

On the stage, the youth group fiddled with a cheap microphone and made it squeal, and everyone groaned pleasantly, the way you do when children remind you of your own.

Elaine's voice carried without effort. "Raffle tickets—two for one if you buy before eight. Thank you, Mr. Kelly, for manning the table." She gave him the box of rolls and a pen with a feather taped to it, a flourish the eighth graders had insisted upon. He wrote names and tore stubs and made change and let the room's order soak into him like a blessing you can hold in your hand.

"Put me down for the quilt," Margaret said, appearing as if she'd always stood three feet off and only stepped forward now that the line thinned. She wore a dress the color of the parish hall walls, a joke only she would have told. "I can't see it on my bed but I could hang it in the hallway and pretend I inherited good taste."

"You came," Robert said, surprised into smiling.

"I go where there's coffee and accountability," she said. "And to make sure you don't forget how to write our last name on a raffle ticket."

He wrote M-A-R-G-A-R-E-T L-E-E neatly, and she watched his hand as if steadiness were a test she kept. "You look like a man who slept four hours," she said, not unkindly.

"Five," he said.

"Then you owe me one," she said, and moved on, already greeting the choir director with the precise amount of warmth required.

From the doorway came the small cool of outside each time it opened. People slipped in and out with the heat clinging to their clothes and their hair lying the way humidity told it to. Somewhere near the kitchen a child began to cry and was folded into someone's shoulder until the sound turned to hiccups.

Robert sold tickets and smiled at jokes and kept his breathing lined up with other people's talk. He could feel, in that way bodies can feel without naming, the empty space that wore a shape. A laugh that was not here. A voice that would have made the room pivot toward it. He hated himself for noting the absence and then hated the hating. Somewhere on 4th Street a jukebox would be sticking on a song and a bartender would be wiping a glass with a cloth that had done its day's work hours ago, and the thought came like a draft under a door he couldn't quite seal.

"Coffee?" Elaine stood with two Styrofoam cups and the smile you save for photographs and ceremonies. Up close he saw the effort at the corner of her mouth. "You're doing wonderfully."

He took a cup. "You are," he said, and meant it.

"Father Donnelly wants to introduce you around after the drawing," she said. "He thinks it's good for the parish to connect faces and names."

"I don't mind being useful," he said.

"I know," she said, and tipped her head, studying him the way she studied a crooked picture until it was straight. "You're pale."

"Fluorescents," he said. "They're merciless."

"They reveal," she said, and moved away before he had to answer that.

The choir sang a hymn too bright for the hour, and people clapped because clapping was easier than listening for the second verse. Robert drank the coffee and let it burn a steady path down. He told himself that if he made it to nine without thinking of Central Avenue he'd be safe until morning. He told himself a lot of things that sounded like rules and worked like superstition.

At eight, Elaine tapped the microphone with a competent forefinger, and it thumped into obedience. "Raffle time," she said. "Thank you, thank you—all of you—for making this parish what it is. We are blessed."

Blessed. The word washed over the room and settled in the corners. Robert drew the first ticket and read a number.

A cheer went up. Pies changed hands. The fishing rod found a boy whose father would take him to Boca Ciega with the pride of teaching him to cast and the quiet ache of a man who wanted his son to know him for something gentle. The coffee basket made the monsignor laugh for real this time. The quilt went to a widow who had made quilts of her own for forty years and cried when she held this one like a woman recognizing her own work made by a stranger's hands.

The evening unspooled toward its end with the slow pleasure of a small success. People gathered coats and children and leftover cookies. The floor began to show itself under scuffed chair legs. Someone turned lights off in corners and left them on over the stage.

Father Donnelly found Robert by the hymnals. "Next Sunday," he said, laying a hand on his shoulder with the weight of blessing and habit. "You'll do the second reading."

"Yes, Father."

"Corinthians," Father Donnelly said, as if it were a prescription. "Medicine. You understand why we put it into a room full of tired people."

Robert nodded. He thought of tiredness as a thing that lived in the body and another that lived in the soul, and how the first could be slept off and the second confessed, and how he had not slept and could not confess.

"Elaine said you'd accept," the priest added, and his smile softened. "You married a woman who makes the right things happen."

"I did," Robert said, and the truth in it made everything else louder for a second.

Elaine shepherded the last of the volunteers toward the kitchen for a quick clean. "If we stack chairs now, we save the maintenance man grief," she said. People stacked chairs.

The clatter made the hall suddenly sound industrial, the way a stage looks when the set is struck and you can see the wings. Robert lifted three chairs at once and felt the small righteous burn in his arms. He stacked them and stacked another set and thought—if I keep carrying, I won't have to think.

When he set the last chair down, he caught sight of Margaret by the door. She had her purse strap over her shoulder and one hand on the jamb. She tilted her chin at him. "Walk me to my car, Mr. Kelly."

He fell into step beside her. Outside, the night pressed close, warm and damp, the parking lot lights throwing islands on the asphalt. Crickets buzzed their constant song under the shrubs that boxed in the parish lawn. The lot smelled faintly of petrol and cut grass.

Margaret stopped by a sensible sedan. She looked at him over the roof like a judge looks over the reading glasses they put on when they want to make sure you notice the eyes. "You're good at rooms," she said. "It's the doors that worry me."

"Meaning?" he asked, buying time.

"Meaning some doors stay closed because a room like this one"—she nodded toward the hall—"depends on it. And some doors don't. You look like a man spending his evenings identifying which are which."

"I go home," he said, and heard how small the defense was.

"Some men take the long way," she said. "I am not your mother or your priest. I'm only the woman who has to keep the calendar straight when men do not. Be careful." She opened her car door. "And tell Elaine the coffee was real coffee. Not that powdered sin she used to order."

He almost laughed. "I will."

She got in, shut the door, and drove off with a wave that didn't make more of itself than necessary. Robert stood a moment longer than made sense, the heat laying a hand on the back of his neck the way a coach does when he means to keep you in the game whether you want to go back in or not.

When he returned to the hall, the echo had deepened. Fewer voices, more clang. Elaine was at the sink in the small kitchen, sleeves rolled, hands in hot water, the practical penitent of a woman who found God as easily in a clean pan as in a psalm. He took the towel without asking and dried. They passed plates like an old married pair in a photograph you find in a drawer and call beautiful even if it wasn't.

"Thank you," she said.

"For drying?" he asked, aiming for light.

"For showing up," she said, and the words were simple and heavier than the plates.

"I always do," he said.

"You always have," she said, and set a pot on the rack as if arranging punctuation.

They finished and flicked switches the way you close a book—one, then another. In the hall, her tote hung heavy with forms and lists. He lifted it for her and felt the weight of small order, of how many little things it takes to keep a place upright. In the dark doorway, she paused and looked up at him.

"You'll do the reading," she said.

"Yes."

"Robert," she said, and his name in her mouth sounded like it had when they were young and waiting for buses and good news—clearer, less freighted. "I know the difference between tired and far away."

He opened his mouth and shut it. "I am here," he said,

because sometimes the least complicated sentence is the best rope you have.

She nodded once. "For now," she said, repeating herself from the kitchen night before, but something in it had changed. It wasn't threat. It wasn't surrender. It was an inventory.

They walked out into the humidity and the space between them felt old and new at once. In the car, she turned the radio low and the announcer told them about weather rolling in from the Gulf like a rumor you could set your watch by. On 9th Avenue a pair of teenagers crossed where they shouldn't with the long legs of people who had never doubted their knees. He waited for them, and Elaine said thank you to the windshield, and the small civility held more weight than it should.

At home, the house had the quiet of a place that had served its purpose all day and wanted nothing more than to be left alone to cool. They set the tote on the hall table. Elaine hung her shawl. He put his keys in the dish and lined them up because his hand needed something to correct. In the living room the lamp they always left on was still on, a square of light on the rug the children would read in tomorrow.

Elaine touched his sleeve. "Sunday," she said.

"Sunday," he said back.

She went upstairs. He stood a long minute in the doorway to the dark kitchen and listened to the refrigerator's small motor and the slow tick of the familiar wall clock and the particular hush of a house that knows the names of its owners.

He thought of the reading. He heard the verse in his head the way a boy hears the ocean in a shell—muffled and undeniable.

Love is patient.

He poured water into a glass and didn't drink it. He set it down and left it there, a small offering to a god he could no longer name without feeling fraudulent. He turned off the lamp and the house deepened around him. On the stairs he placed his feet with care, as if the drumbeat of them might wake something that would not be put back to sleep.

In the bedroom, Elaine lay with her back to his side of the bed, breathing, not pretending to be asleep but committed to it. He undressed in the slow careful way a man does when he does not want to be heard. When he slid under the sheet, the mattress gave that small sound a bed makes when it receives a familiar weight.

He faced the ceiling. He closed his eyes. He opened them. On the inside of his lids, the parish hall lights hung without their fixture, bright coins. The quilt's tiny squares patterning his sight. Margaret's look across the roof of the car. Elaine's hand in steam.

He turned his head toward the window. Somewhere to the east, the Pier would be standing at the water's edge, absurd and permanent, as if concrete could preach. Farther inland, on 34th, the vacancy signs would be rehearsing their arguments to any man who bothered to listen. He tried not to, and still he heard them. He could not make the city stop speaking just because he wanted the night quiet.

He counted breaths. He told himself Sunday would come and he would stand there and read and the room would believe him. He told himself that would be enough to carry him the rest of the way across whatever this was. He told himself many things. Some were true. Most were useful.

When sleep finally found him, it did not keep him. He woke at three to the sound of rain practicing on the roof, light, then a little harder, then deciding against it. Beside him, Elaine stirred and settled. He lay on his back and let the dark do what it does—take the edges off and sharpen the center. In the space where night puts its hand on a man's sternum and waits for him to admit the softest truth, he admitted nothing out loud.

He pictured the lectern. He pictured the word patient. He thought of how patience and waiting are not the same thing. He thought of doors.

# 4

# LOVE IS PATIENT

Sunday wore its good clothes. The sky came on clear and pale, the kind of morning the bay keeps for itself and shares with anyone willing to be quiet. The Kellys walked up the Cathedral steps in a row—Elaine with her choir binder tucked to her side, the children fighting their fidgets, Robert smoothing a cuff he'd already smoothed.

Incense had been burning long enough to soften the edges of the nave. Light broke through stained glass and laid colored shapes over shoulders, a patchwork congregation. On the lectern the missal sat open to the reading he knew by heart from the moment Father Donnelly had said the word. Corinthians. Love explained in a voice that didn't know exhaustion.

The first hymn rose—firm, familiar—and Robert found the melody without thinking. His throat felt better carrying other people's words. He followed the notes until the final chord settled like a benediction over wood and stone.

"Second reading," the deacon said, and Robert left the pew and walked down the center aisle. He could feel

Elaine's gaze steadying his back the way a hand steadies a child on skates. The steps to the sanctuary were polished by years and he took them in the rhythm of men who don't look at their feet.

"At the time," he began, and the microphone made him larger than he felt. His own voice surprised him, low, even, trained by courtrooms and radios and kitchens where a man reads a bedtime story slower than the day would like. "Love is patient, love is kind..."

He kept his eye on the page and not on the room. The words landed the way rain lands on a pier—soft at first, then all at once everywhere. He kept reading and heard himself anyway. Not jealous or boastful. Not arrogant or rude. Love bears all things, believes all things. The congregation breathed as one animal and he held the line steady, amazed that his voice could behave while something under his ribs did not.

When he finished, he closed the book gently, because gentleness counts in small ways, and walked back to his seat. Elaine's hand found his. It was warm, dry, the same hand that had carried pies and turned hymnals and pressed his shoulder last night in a kitchen full of steam. He squeezed once. She squeezed back, and in the silent exchange he could hear twenty years of promises adding up into a number that wouldn't balance if he kept borrowing.

Father Donnelly's homily was about work and mercy, about how a city needs both to stand up. Robert tried to listen, but the line that stuck was from the end, where the priest always tucked the practical lesson. "Patience is not postponement," he said. "It's endurance with love in it." The words drew a neat circle around Robert's chest and pulled.

After Mass they passed through the receiving line hand in hand, a picture of what a good Sunday looks like:

respectability without stiffness. "Beautiful reading," said a man from the men's club. "Steady," said Mrs. Genaro. "See you Friday," said the monsignor, because parish calendars never slept. Elaine glowed in the careful way of a woman who knows praise should be deflected toward God and the committee.

On the steps, a breeze moved over them and children ran in figure eights while parents grabbed at small sleeves. Margaret appeared from the side aisle like a footnote someone had forgotten and then remembered was the most important part. "Well read," she said, and in the two words he heard the thing she wasn't saying. Her eyes held him a second too long. Then she looked at Elaine and smiled a different smile. "The fundraiser was a run of good stitches. It'll hold."

"Thank you for coming," Elaine said.

"I come for the coffee," Margaret said, deadpan. "The God is a bonus."

It made Elaine laugh, which seemed to please Margaret more than anything else would have. She excused herself with a gesture that was almost a salute, and the crowd absorbed her as if the city understood the uses of a person like that and didn't need to make a fuss.

Back at the house, Sunday laid out its comforts like picnic food. Roast in the oven. Baseball on low in the living room. Matthew crowded his father with the plane again, and this time the wing held as if it had decided to trust them. Anna practiced a hymn on the piano with one hand, the left waiting for the day it would be brave. Elaine stood at the sink humming, not the tune from Mass but another one he recognized from when they were young and leaned on the railing of a different pier and said things into the wind that sounded like certainty.

He tried to let the afternoon claim him. He turned the radio down and up and settled on down. He read the paper front to back and couldn't recount a line. He washed plates and dried them. He stepped out to the yard and looked up at a sky that was already thinking about the evening storm.

At four, a phone call came—Marlene Greer, voice cool, asking Elaine if she might borrow the parish chairs for a charity thing she was "whipped into." They talked in the cadence of women who know the same men and not the same marriages. When Elaine hung up she looked at Robert, head tilted.

"She says Plant City is 'stifling' this time of year," Elaine said.

"Plant City is stifling every time of year," he said, and the smile arrived late, like a train with a bad schedule.

Elaine's gaze lingered. "Did you ever think about living farther inland?"

"Not since I learned which way the wind comes from," he said, and the line was light enough to pass as banter if you didn't stand too close to it.

Evening took its chair. The storm rolled in from the bay with the quiet arrogance of weather that knows you won't cancel plans over it. Dinner was easy, plates scraped, kids bathed, pajamas, one book and then half of another because half is a bargain you make with sleepy children when what you really want is for your house to agree to stop needing you for a while.

They said prayers at the foot of the beds. Matthew jumbled his list of saints with the starting lineup; Anna asked for protection for "Dad's voice" and "Mom's clipboard," and Elaine laughed without sound. When the lights were out, the house made the sounds houses make—pipes thinking, wood remembering day heat, distant cars stitching the neighborhood to the rest of the town.

Downstairs, Elaine poured two small glasses of wine and set one on the table in front of him. "To a good Sunday," she said.

"To the same," he said, and they drank and were quiet.

"You read well," she added finally.

"I know how to read well," he said.

"I know you do," she said. She stood and gathered the glasses and his thanks, and the ritual felt both saving and false. The radio murmured about a low-pressure system that might come to nothing. The announcer used the word "unsettled," and the word lay down beside him and refused to move.

After dishes, she touched his arm. "Will you lock up?" she asked, and kissed his cheek. "I'm going to bed early. You should come soon."

"I'll check the back door," he said. It sounded like faith when he said it. It sounded like delay when she heard it.

He walked the house. Thumbed the latch by the kitchen. Flicked the porch light off and watched the backyard dim into that rich dark Florida makes in summer, thick with the hum of things that have no interest in human schedules. He stood with his hand on the switch, listening to his own steadiness.

Upstairs, the bedroom lamp went out. He pictured Elaine turning the page of her book, then admitting defeat, then setting it down in the neat stack that made sense of her nightstand. He thought about climbing the stairs, loosing his tie, telling the truth. The thought made the hallway longer.

He took his keys from the dish.

The motion was small. The sound was not. Even the soft

clink announced itself in the hour's quiet. He waited—one, two heartbeats—for a voice from above. Nothing. Houses understand the limits of their authority. He opened the front door and stood for a second with one foot inside and one foot out, like a child testing pool water. The humidity climbed his collar like a hand.

He told himself he was driving nowhere. He told himself a drive has no destination until it does. He told himself, out loud in the dark, "I'm just going." It sounded foolish and honest in equal measure.

The Buick turned over lazy, then decided to help. He backed out with the practiced caution of a man who believes he is careful. On the street, he pointed the car away from the bay on purpose and turned toward it anyway two blocks later. He took 22nd to 9th to 4th as if the steering wheel had preferences. The city opened like a palm. Sodium lamps threw their tired halos. Signs buzzed. Neon bristled.

He passed The Pier on purpose. He passed it the way a faithful man passes a church on a weeknight—eyes front, not stopping, a small bow he wouldn't admit to. He took the long way around downtown to pretend he didn't know where he wanted to be. He turned on the radio and turned it off again. The windshield caught a few exploratory drops and then cleared, as if the weather had changed its mind.

He turned on 4th.

You didn't have to look for Hank's Hideaway if you already knew where the clever sign didn't point. The windows were dark enough to pass inspection. The door looked like any narrow door on any narrow block. A man smoked outside with one shoe flattened at the heel. Another man said something that made the first smile without moving his mouth. The jukebox had a reputation for working when the rest of the city didn't.

Robert parked a half block down beneath a streetlamp that made his hood a dull pewter. He left the engine running. He turned it off. He put the keys in his pocket and took them out and put them back in like he could choose a version of himself with his hand. The air smelled like fryer oil from a diner and the salt rearranged by a day's wind. Somewhere a bottle clinked against another bottle and sounded like a cheap toast.

He watched the door. It opened and closed twice while he sat there. A pair of sailors went in laughing the easy laugh of men who intend to go further than they say. A man in a suit came out, loosened his tie with the relief of a rabbit stepping into a hole it knows. No one looked down the block at a Buick with a respectable man behind the wheel. The city has better things to do with its eyes.

He stepped out.

The heat met him with a familiarity that was almost kindness. He closed the car door gently because slamming would have felt like admitting something. His shoes made a sound on the sidewalk like punctuation—periods, not exclamation points. He could feel a pulse in his neck that belonged to a boy he didn't think he'd see again.

Halfway down the block he stopped. The door to Hank's was fifteen steps away. He stood at fourteen. He looked down at his hands as if they were not his, then up at the sky that offered nothing but its ordinary dark. He took one step and heard the city change key.

He could turn around. He could. He knew the movements. He could trace them with his finger like a prayer on a page.

He took another step.

The man with the cigarette glanced at him and then away, as if there were a code about granting strangers the gift of pretending. The jukebox inside hit the chorus of something he knew without knowing why. It sounded like a cheap promise and a true one.

He reached for the handle.

The chrome was warm from other hands. In the reflection he saw himself small and distorted, then larger as his fingers closed.

From his pocket, the keys pressed a shape into his thigh that felt exactly like a life.

He pulled the door an inch and the seam let go a thread of cool air and the smell of beer and cheap cologne and a kind of safety men invent when they cannot find the real kind.

He didn't step through. Not yet. He held it—door, breath, hour—as if he could keep everything suspended by will.

Behind him, a car rolled through the intersection, its headlights sweeping the storefront like a searchlight that had grown tired of catching people. Far off, the bay made its constant sound. The city drew a breath and waited to see which story he would tell about himself next.

Robert pushed the door another inch.

# 5

# THE DOOR THAT GIVES

The door gave like a secret—you didn't need to push hard, you only needed to want to. Robert stepped into the narrow dark and let the quiet guard at the threshold swing it shut behind him. The room took him in and didn't look up.

Hank's Hideaway wasn't much to see with the lights on, which was why they never were. Neon signs—BEER, OPEN, a blue marlin frozen in perpetual leap—did the work of decoration. The bar ran along the left, wood worn to a soft shine by elbows and apologies. Two pool tables toward the back, their felt dim islands under green shades. A jukebox against the far wall hummed even between songs, as if remembering something it couldn't quite say. Smoke hung polite and persistent. The place smelled like old citrus rinds and new regret.

The bartender glanced over with professional indifference that read as kindness if you needed it to. "What'll it be," he said, already reaching.

"Club soda," Robert said, voice lower than the room required. "Lime."

"Classy," the bartender said without judgment. He slid the glass across and went back to the men who were building a case with quarters at the pool table.

Robert took a stool two down from the end and turned half toward the room like a man waiting for a train he couldn't admit he'd scheduled. The first sip was as cold as he wanted the night to be. He watched without staring: the sailor with his cap tucked in his back pocket; a man in a suit whose tie had made it as far as his breastbone; a pair of boys pretending they were older, failing comfortably. He breathed and let the noise put a hand on his shoulder and keep him in the chair.

A song he recognized dropped into the room—strings cheap and sincere, a voice rasping about a woman with a name that sounded like a street and a promise. The jukebox light shifted and threw honey-colored bars along the mirror behind the bottles. In the glass, Robert saw himself at an angle—tired, neat, almost convincing. He looked like a man who could be mistaken for a better one if he kept still.

"Rob."

The word came low enough to be a choice. He turned without the flinch he felt.

Tommy stood a foot away, hands empty, tie loose, sleeves rolled twice. The light favored his mouth more than his eyes; the grin was smaller than the one he used on juries. He held his body like a door he could close if he had to.

"I didn't think you'd—" Tommy began, then stopped, because finishing would turn the sentence into a verdict.

"I almost didn't," Robert said.

Tommy nodded as if they were discussing weather. He took the stool to Robert's right, leaving a careful inch of air that might as well have been a yard. He raised two fingers to the bartender. "Club soda," he said, glancing sideways with a humor so dry it cracked. "Lime."

They did the thing men do in rooms where admission is the only confession that counts: they looked at the bottles, not each other. Sipped. Set glasses down gently, like the wood could bruise.

"You read this morning," Tommy said after the jukebox changed its mind.

"I did."

"Was it patience or kindness," Tommy asked, "that stuck in your throat."

"Endurance," Robert said, before he could talk himself out of it.

Tommy's laugh was small and painful and kind. "We keep thinking we invented our own trouble," he said, "and then Corinthians shows up like a smug cousin."

"Don't," Robert said, and didn't know which part he was answering—the joke, the scripture, the recognition in Tommy's voice that made the room tilt.

They sat. The bar gave them cover. Men argued behind them about whether to bank the eight or risk the cut and the laughter came in on the off-beats, warm, not cruel. Someone told a story about a busted alternator as if it were a parable. The bartender wiped the same patch of wood three times and remembered not to ask questions he couldn't unhear.

"I saw you from the window," Tommy said, looking at the mirror. "At the pier the other night."

Robert set his glass down too carefully. "I thought I was good at being alone."

"You are," Tommy said. "That's the problem."

Silence found them again, but it had changed shape. It

wasn't empty now, it was full, like the pause before a verdict that everyone knows and no one wants recorded.

"You don't have to narrate this," Robert said finally, because naming is a kind of touching and he couldn't afford either.

"I'm not," Tommy said. "I'm just—here."

He meant it. It was the plainest sentence in the room and it rang anyway. Robert reached for his glass and found his hand steady. The jukebox dropped a Motown cut that didn't belong and the whole bar tried to remember how to move to it without promising more than their knees could deliver. On the far table, a ball fell wrong and rolled right and a chorus of "no, no—yes" lifted and died.

Robert let out a breath he hadn't labeled. "We are very stupid men," he said, and the words landed gentle instead of cruel. "And we are not boys."

"Both are true," Tommy said. "And not enough."

They looked at each other then, because there comes a point when the mirror won't do. Up close, Tommy's eyes held too many nights. Up close, Robert felt every year he had not wanted to count. He recognized in the other man's face the specific relief of not talking yourself through your own door alone.

Tommy glanced at the jukebox. "That thing still takes a punch to behave," he said, and stood, a small reprieve dressed as a joke. He crossed the room, rapped the side with his knuckles like a man greeting an old dog, fed quarters. When the next song came, it came clean, a slow one that sat down quietly beside you and stayed. Robert watched him the way a drowning man watches a boat, embarrassed to be seen, too far along to pretend he didn't need the sight.

On his way back, Tommy stopped long enough to answer

a question from the bartender about Monday's hearing. He spoke low and quick and easy, the way he did when the law was a language he could choose. Then he took the stool again and didn't turn it toward Robert, which felt like mercy.

"Greer," the bartender called, making the name a greeting and a warning.

"Yeah," Tommy said, not looking up.

"You're good for your tab."

"Not tonight," Tommy said, and the bartender went back to glassware with a nod that meant we both understand tomorrow.

Robert put a bill under his glass as if it were a bandage. He didn't count it. Tommy saw the motion and didn't comment. Small dignities can be shared if you don't try to name them.

"You should go," Tommy said, after a while. The sentence rode no judgement. It sounded like a friend saying you've had enough when you've had none.

"I know," Robert said, and stayed one heartbeat longer than made sense. Then he put his hand on the bar and pushed himself up the way you do when you've been sitting with the wrong thoughts and your legs need instruction.

Tommy kept his eyes on the mirror. "Tomorrow," he said, and the word took no position—promise, threat, weather.

Robert nodded and didn't trust himself to shape a noise. He set his empty on the rubber mat, because order is a muscle you can flex even when you're weak. He walked past the pool tables and the jukebox and the door that didn't ask for farewells. The neon pushed a little color into his shirt as if to mark him for the street.

Outside, the night had thickened the way Florida nights do when they decide to be generous. Traffic on 4th whispered tires on wet from a block where the diner still did eggs for men who lived on their own time. Robert stood a second and let the air rearrange him. He hadn't crossed any border you could see. He had still left and arrived.

Halfway to his car, a voice said his name the way you say it when you're checking whether the person you think you know is the person you actually know.

"Mr. Kelly?"

He turned. The kid was lanky and young in that way that seems like it hurts the bones. Denim jacket, hair too long for church, not long enough for rebellion. He held a bakery crate against his hip and a cigarette badly, as if it belonged to a friend. Robert placed the face a second before the name. Margaret's sister's boy. Danny Lee. He'd seen him at Christmas once, orbiting the punch bowl with the polite concentration of a new planet.

"Danny," Robert said, and made it sound like a hello you could explain anywhere.

"Didn't mean to—" The kid gestured with the cigarette and looked at his own hand like it had betrayed him. "I deliver to the diner. They're short. Aunt Margaret said it'd keep me from playing cards."

"It will," Robert said neutrally. "Cards are a poor investment."

Danny nodded, grateful for the script. His eyes were kind and sharp the way a certain kind of boy's are before the world dulls one or the other. "Nice to see you," he said, and meant it because he didn't know how not to.

"You too," Robert said.

They performed the small choreography of men letting each other off a hook neither had claimed. Danny shifted the crate. Robert smiled a fraction. They both looked toward the diner, toward the bar, toward the street simultaneously and then at their shoes, letting the geometry apportion blame to the pavement.

"Tell your aunt," Robert said, "the coffee at St. Jude's has been redeemed."

Danny's mouth twitched. "She'll say it was under her administration."

"It was," Robert said, and they both almost laughed, and the almost was mercy.

Robert reached his car. The keys found the lock like they'd been born to it. He sat with his hands on the wheel and waited for the blood in his head to stop writing his pulse on the inside of his skull. In the rearview, Danny crossed, careful with the crate, a kid doing a good job. Beyond him, Hank's door opened and closed as if the building breathed. The jukebox dropped a new song into the street like a coin skittered across a counter—bright, brief, somebody else's.

He started the car. He told himself he would drive a different route home and failed. The Pier appeared because it always did when you wanted to prove to yourself you weren't looking. He didn't stop. He didn't need to. The decision had already been made; the body follows the mind at whatever speed it can survive.

At the house, the porch light made a small theater of the front steps. He turned the engine off and listened to the cooling tick, a sound like a clock forgiving itself. The neighborhood was dark the way decent places are—kids asleep, dogs convinced of borders, sprinklers spending the last of the water. He slid the key into the lock and then took it out and held it, as if the metal might warm enough to learn something.

Inside, the hallway had the hush of late rooms. He set his keys in the dish without ceremony and stood long enough to hear his own breath settle. Upstairs, the house kept Elaine's secrets as faithfully as it kept his. He climbed, careful on the parts of the steps that creak, moving like a man visiting his own life for the night.

In bed, he lay on his back and let the ceiling perform the trick where it looks like sky if you need it to. He closed his eyes. The bar followed him anyway—not the smell, not the smoke, not the jukebox—just the sentence Tommy had used and refused to sharpen.

Tomorrow.

He didn't pray. He didn't not. He let the word hang where a prayer would. When sleep came, it came in shreds, and between them he heard the city making a deal with him he would not honor, and he forgave himself for accepting anyway.

# 6

# MORNING AFTER

Morning pretended nothing had happened, and the world agreed to play along. The same light came through the blinds. The same sound of sprinklers on the neighbor's lawn. The same voice on the radio—weather, traffic, a song half-familiar. Only Robert knew the difference, and even he tried to forget it.

He shaved slow, careful, as though steadiness could be re-learned with a razor. Elaine hummed from the kitchen. Coffee drifted down the hall, that same dependable roast she'd favored for years. He tied his tie by muscle memory. He looked, for all purposes, like a man leaving for work.

"Margaret called," Elaine said when he came in. "She said there's an early meeting about the new client."

"Good," he said, sitting for the first cup. "She runs that place."

Elaine smiled. "She runs you."

He smiled back, because that was the right response. She poured his coffee, kissed his cheek, and looked at him just a beat too long. Then she turned back to the stove, humming again, and he exhaled.

He left before the kids came down, before routine could ask him to stay longer than his alibi.

———

The drive to the office was the same route, same lights, same Gulf wind sneaking through the vent. But everything looked sharper, like the city had cleaned its mirrors overnight. He saw every sign, every window. The street felt new, dangerous for its clarity.

At Kelly & Greer, the door groaned its usual greeting. Margaret was there already, typing with her morning precision.

"Morning, Mr. Kelly," she said, without looking up.

"Morning."

He set his briefcase down and checked the day's docket. A probate review, two phone calls, one hearing that Greer could handle. The clock read eight-forty.

Margaret stopped typing. "You all right? You look like you ran into the sunrise."

"I'm fine."

"Sure," she said. "Tommy's running late. He called. Voice sounded—rough."

Robert kept his face neutral. "Big weekend."

"Guess so."

She went back to her keys. The sound was the same as always, but somehow it filled more space.

When Tommy arrived, he didn't bother with the grin. Just nodded at Margaret, then at Robert, and went straight to his office. The door didn't quite close, and that was its own message.

Robert sat down. He signed papers. He dictated a letter. He tried to let the day rebuild itself around him. But there was that pulse again—the echo of neon, the hum of a jukebox, the sound of his name said softly and wrong.

At eleven, Margaret dropped a file on his desk. "Danny's delivering the bakery order for the staff meeting," she said. "Be polite. He thinks you're some kind of gentleman."

The paper slid from his hand. "Danny?"

"Lee," she said, watching him. "Why? He run into you last night?"

He took longer than necessary to answer. "At the diner. Briefly."

Her eyes narrowed just slightly. "You been down there this week?"

He forced a smile. "Needed air."

"You and half the city," she said, but her tone had changed. Softer. Sadder. "Watch your step, Robert. There's gossip in this town that grows like mold."

He nodded. "I'll mind the humidity."

"Do," she said. "It ruins more than shoes."

She left the door open on purpose this time.

———

Tommy didn't speak until noon. "Lunch?" he said, from the doorway.

Robert looked up. "Café?"

Tommy shook his head. "Not today."

They ended up walking anyway—past the courthouse, past the pawn shop with the same window display every season, down toward the bay where the air smelled like metal and salt. They talked about clients, cases, small things. The kind of talk that papers over everything else.

At the water, Tommy stopped. "Danny Lee saw you."

"I know."

"He told Margaret."

"I know."

Tommy kicked a shell into the surf. "So now she knows. Which means someone else will know. That's how it works."

"I didn't go in there to be seen."

"I didn't say you did."

They stood there a while. The wind lifted Tommy's hair, dropped it again. A pelican dove and came up with nothing.

"You could still step back," Tommy said. "Before anyone writes it down."

Robert looked at the horizon, at the line where water met sky and refused to blend. "Step back to where."

Tommy didn't answer.

They walked back without talking. At the corner, Tommy peeled off toward a lunch counter, leaving Robert with the street and the sun. He felt like he'd walked out of his own life and couldn't find the door back in.

———

By evening, clouds had stacked over the bay, dark and slow-moving. Elaine met him at the door, towel in hand.

"Dinner's late," she said. "Storm's coming. The radio says lightning over Clearwater."

"Storms always miss us," he said.

She turned to look out the window. "Not always."

He hung his jacket and looked at her reflection in the glass. The woman who had shared his house, his children, his prayers. The one who never asked the wrong questions because she knew how much damage the right ones could do.

He wanted to tell her everything and nothing at once. Instead, he said, "I might be late tomorrow. The Jenkins case."

She nodded, still watching the horizon. "Take an umbrella."

When he kissed her temple, she didn't move away, but she didn't lean in either. The smell of rain was close enough to taste.

———

At his desk that night, the city humming outside, Robert stared at the legal pad in front of him. The pen lay still. He wrote two words—"Hank's Hideaway"—then crossed them out. Beneath, he wrote "Tomorrow," and left it there, a single word heavier than all the others.

He turned off the light.

Outside, thunder rolled across the bay like something too large to name.

# 7

## STORM INSTRUCTIONS

The storm announced itself the way trouble does in Florida—first as a rumor on the radio, then as a change in the color of the afternoon. The heat went flat. The air thickened until the skin felt like a wick. By three, the sky had turned the wrong green over the bay, and the palm fronds along Central held their breath.

Kelly & Greer kept the lamps lit and pretended the light was enough. The fans wobbled a little harder. Margaret watched the windows the way a ship's officer watches the horizon—professionally, already doing the math.

"At half past, I'm sending you both home," she said, fingers still moving on the keys. "I won't have my name attached to two men electrocuted by optimism."

"Optimism has served us," Tommy said from the doorway, but even his voice had lowered to the register people use in hospitals and storms.

"Optimism can take the bus," she said. "Lightning rides for free."

Outside, the first curtain of rain came across 4th Street so cleanly you could see where dry ended and wet began.

Cars flicked wipers on late, as if modesty had kept them from noticing. The café pulled its chalkboard inside. A kid on a bike made a sprint for the awning and didn't make it, and when he laughed at his own bad timing, the sound came up the stairwell and into the office like a dare.

The lights blinked. Came back. Blinked again and stayed. Everyone looked briefly at the ceiling as if the plaster could promise anything.

"Files," Margaret said. "Shut. Covered. Away from the windows. We'll not have Mr. Greer's brilliances turned to papier-mâché."

"My brilliances are waterproof," Tommy said, collecting folders anyway. "Mr. Kelly's are laminated in principle."

Robert slid a stack into the cabinet with the care of a man putting away good dishes before a party turns. He checked the latch twice and then felt foolish for checking a third time. On the sill, a thin line of dust had gathered—the kind of domestic neglect that makes a place feel honest.

Thunder rolled in—far, then near, then exactly above. The building flinched and pretended it hadn't.

"Now," Margaret said, standing. "Go."

"Greer's driving a convertible today," Robert said.

"It has a top," Tommy said, noncommittal.

"It has a prayer," Margaret said, and pointed to the door. "Shoo."

They made it as far as the landing when the sky emptied with intent. The hallway went dim in the way old buildings do when noon becomes night. On the first-floor stoop, men from the tailor shop and the cigar place collected under the canopy—shirtsleeves, hats turned low, the posture of men resigned to weather's rights. Down the block, a streetlight flicked on wrong and threw its cone onto rain like a spotlight on beads.

"Wait it," Tommy said, stepping under the building's shallow eyebrow of shelter. He shook his hair once like a dog who knew he'd still be wet.

Robert joined him, shoulder to shoulder with an inch of air. The rain came hard enough to raise mist where it hit the street. Water found the low spots and made quick opinions of them. A car crept through the intersection, the bow wave small and sincere.

"Elaine will have called me a fool by now," Robert said, half to himself.

"She'd be right about the weather," Tommy said. "Not the rest."

Robert kept his eyes on the street. "Don't."

"Name it?" Tommy asked, not pushing.

"Make it smaller," Robert said.

They stood with that, breathing the same damp air. A peal of thunder cracked so close the glass chimed in the door behind them. Every man under the awning made the same face—a flinch turned into a smile to keep dignity. The rain found a leak in the gutter and drafted itself into a steady drip near Robert's shoe. He moved half a step. Tommy matched him without thinking, a small choreography they could have denied under oath.

"Power'll go," one of the cigar men said cheerfully. "It always does when you've got pork on the stove."

"Then go home," his friend said.

"And get killed crossing 34th? My wife will forgive the pork. The bus won't forgive my body."

Robert felt the laugh tug at him and didn't let it show. Lightning tore the sky again, and for a breath the street was a black-and-white photograph—faces drained to bone, rain like lines etched with a needle, the inverted pyramid at the end of Central a ghost geometry against the bright. He saw it, felt it write itself on some tender place, and when the color returned he couldn't quite call the street the same one.

"You ever think about what the bay remembers?" Tommy asked softly, without looking at him. "Storm to storm? How it just—holds?"

"Water forgets," Robert said.

"Does it?"

They didn't move. The rain eased, then gathered itself meaner, then eased again. A bus splashed the curb and a small wave wet the toes of everyone's shoes. No one swore. Weather absolves carelessness.

"What if this is the part where we decide," Tommy said, and the sentence was so mild that it took Robert a second to understand the weight of it.

Robert swallowed. "Decide to what."

"To stop being men who pretend the weather is the only thing happening."

The word men sat between them like a plate set on a table during an argument—practical, a little hard, the sort of thing you could slide away if you wanted to speak kinder. Robert watched the rain blow slant and hit the café window. He pictured Elaine in their kitchen, checking the stove and the children, counting the seconds between flash and rumble the way her mother had taught her.

"You think talking names it," he said.

"I think not talking does," Tommy said, so quietly Robert had to tilt his head a fraction to hear. "I think silence is a kind of oath and I'm tired of the wrong promises."

Another flash. Another tearing roll right on top of it.

"You'll get us drowned," Robert said, meaning you'll get us found.

Tommy leaned his shoulder against the brick, an easy posture that looked practiced and wasn't. "I'll get us wet."

Robert could feel the center of himself having an argument the edges had already lost. The storm took a long angry breath and loosened, the way a man loosens after he's said what he's been meaning to say for an hour. The street became merely flooded instead of biblical. The cigar men shook themselves, declared a tie with God, and dashed for their doors.

"Go," Robert said, before the small window closed and courage curdled into common sense. "Before Margaret sees you drive with the top down and writes your obituary."

Tommy smiled without triumph. "Tonight," he said, too low for anyone else to own. "Not Hank's."

Robert didn't say yes. He didn't say no. He watched the rain try to become mist and fail. "The pier," he said.

"The pier," Tommy echoed, and the word had the shape of a promise men sign with their breathing first.

They split for their cars. The sky gave one more rumble like a parting insult, then let them have the street. Robert drove slow in the shallow-rivered lanes, the tires finding the path other tires had made, wipers beating a time his chest tried to borrow. He passed the café with its lights a little dimmer, the tailor shop closed early, the arcade window flickering like a bad dream. He didn't look at the clock. He didn't need a number to tell him he was late to something.

At 4th, a limb blocked the right lane and a man in a good shirt moved it by degrees, the way decent men do when no one tells them to. Robert pulled over, put on his flashers, and helped. "Thank you," the man said, short of breath and gratitude. "World's wet today."

"Tomorrow too," Robert said, and felt the sentence stick.

By the time he crossed 2nd and could see the water, the rain had fallen into a steadier habit. The bay took it without comment. The inverted pyramid hung wrong and beautiful at the end of the road, a promise that never kept the kind you expected. He pulled into the municipal lot and let the car idle, watching the boards darken under the rhythm of the drops.

Someone—three someones—walked out on the pier with their jackets up like makeshift roofs. A gull stood on one leg and looked unimpressed by the species that required all this equipment to stay upright. The wind had found its song and sung it in the wires and the motel signs and the flag halyards, one long note braided.

He didn't get out. Not yet. He sat with the engine running and the radio low—a ballgame somewhere in a calmer city where the storm was an idea. He could see the door to the bait shop swing and shut, swing and shut. A boy ran and slid and got scolded and ran again. A couple stood too close the way couples do under weather. The rain made halos in the puddles and broke them.

He cut the engine. The quiet that followed felt like a knife sliding back into its sheath.

He got out.

The first breath he took tasted like tin and salt; he swallowed it greedily, as if air were a drink you had to pay for now and wanted your money's worth. He walked to the rail and put his palms on the cold wet, letting the water soak the cuffs of his jacket because some costs are easier to pay in public. The bay reached right up to touch the underside of the boards and didn't ask permission.

He didn't see Tommy. That was good. That was terrible. He stood, felt the pier move under him in that slow animal way, the wood flexing with the water's opinion, and let his heartbeat find the larger rhythm.

Time is different in rain. It's marked by drops, not by seconds. He stayed long enough for a small flood to find his shoes and then recede when the wind shifted. He stayed long enough to decide he would go. He stayed one minute longer than that.

When he turned, the storm had changed the light to something like evening. Figures moved along the boards— fewer now, mostly men who had never minded getting wet because water doesn't judge. He stepped back into the parking lot and shook his sleeves once, a gesture that admitted nothing.

Across the way, beneath the shelter of the closed snack stand, a shape leaned—hands in pockets, collar up. Tommy. Not close. Not far. Watching the water like a man who could make a life of it. The sight was a relief and a problem so large it didn't fit under the name.

They didn't meet in the middle. They closed the distance as if they'd planned it—Robert angling left, Tommy right, arriving at a corner of shade where neither would get soaked and both could pretend practicality chose the spot. They stood with the edge between them: wood, water, a storm that had decided not to end yet.

"You came," Tommy said.

"You said tonight," Robert said.

"I did," Tommy said, and looked at the water again like it was telling him something in a language he nearly knew. "Hank's is a bad place for men who don't want to lie about what they're doing."

"This is better?" Robert asked.

"This is honest," Tommy said.

The rain softened a notch. A line of light, weak and tired but trying, appeared along the western horizon like the cuff of a shirt you hadn't noticed under a coat. The wind turned and the smell of the city—hot asphalt, damp stucco, a thousand dinners—came out to meet the salt.

"We can still call it weather," Robert said. "We can say we're only here because the storm asked."

"We can," Tommy agreed. "We can say anything that keeps us standing."

They let the words sit and felt how little language can do when a body has already decided what story it wants to be in. A fishing line out on the beam plucked, a man cursed softly, a woman laughed once and then stopped because the sound didn't fit the room. The gull finally put its other foot down.

"I can't cross every line tonight," Robert said, voice low enough to keep the sentence from echoing.

"I'm not asking you to," Tommy said. "I'm asking you not to lie to yourself about which ones you already did."

Lightning stitched a ragged seam to the east and didn't bother with thunder. The two men watched it and didn't pretend they were admiring weather. Under the shelter, the concrete smelled like the ocean had tried to live indoors and given up.

"We'll see each other tomorrow," Tommy said.

"We will," Robert said.

"And after," Tommy said, not as a question.

Robert didn't answer. He let the rain answer for him—soft now, almost a veil, as if the city had agreed to give them five more minutes of being no one in particular.

They walked back toward the lot together and separated three strides before cars, as if the choreography had been taught at birth. Robert opened his door, sat, started the engine, then turned the key back just so he could sit with the quiet again. When he looked up, Tommy was already turning onto 2nd, his taillights two small red commas in a sentence the bay would keep revising.

Robert drove home by the long route. The storm

followed at a gentleman's distance. He parked under the yellow wash of the streetlight and wiped his palms on his trousers before he went in. The sound the lock made accepting the key was too loud in the sleeping house.

Upstairs, Elaine lay curled on her side, a book facedown near her hand. He stood there and watched the rise and fall of the woman he had promised. In the mirror, he looked like a man who could be forgiven if he stopped now, while stopping still counted. He switched off the hall light and told himself the morning would be kinder.

Outside, the storm made no promises. The bay turned in its sleep and kept what it remembered.

# 8

# RETURN TO THE PIER

T he storm left a film on the city, as if the bay had exhaled and everything had caught the breath. By nightfall the streets were dry again, but the air remembered. The neon along 4th blinked like a tired eye. Robert told himself the day had been ordinary—papers moved, calls returned, a judge said something caustic and correct—and hearing it didn't make it true.

He waited until the house took on its late quiet. Elaine's lamp went out at ten. The children sighed in their rooms with the loose, shameless sleep of the young. He stood in the kitchen long enough to feel like a man deciding between water and wine and chose keys.

Outside, the Buick made the agreeable sound of something you can still control. He drove the long way, past the diner, past Hank's, not looking and looking anyway. The night wore a thin wind. The inverted pyramid at the end of Central was lit in that particular municipal glow that made it look both sacred and bureaucratic.

He parked in the municipal lot without pretending surprise. The boards of the pier were dark from last night's rain and lighter where the day had worked on them. A few fishermen worked the rail in the far lights, their language spare and ocean-shaped. A couple walked with their elbows brushing; a boy ran ahead and waited, ran ahead and waited.

Robert went to the seaward side and put both hands on the rail as if the bay required proof of intention. Water made its soft argument under the boards. He tried to tally the day —what he'd said and not said, the way his voice had behaved around Elaine's name, the small new silences in the office—and the ledger refused to balance.

"Rob."

He didn't flinch. He turned like a man who had rehearsed it and found it still hurt.

Tommy stood to his left, a step back, close enough that the wind brought his soap and his day. No tie tonight. The sleeves rolled. The tired at the eyes not from work. He nodded once, small and grateful, as if they'd kept an appointment neither had set.

"Thought you might," Tommy said.

"I told myself I wouldn't," Robert said.

"Liar," Tommy said, almost kind.

They stood with the rail between them and the water, letting the bay's dark convince them the conversation could be temporary. The hum from the bait shop sign filled the silence the way a distant train does in other cities.

"Do you know the worst part," Robert said, not sure he'd meant to speak. "I can do almost everything right. I can buy flowers on birthdays. I can read Corinthians without my voice breaking. I can walk past a door and never touch the handle. Almost everything. It's the almost that kills a man."

Tommy looked out over the water and tipped his head like he was listening for a buoy bell. "I have never been impressed by men who do everything right," he said. "They're usually standing on someone else's back. The almost is where we tell the truth."

"Don't make it noble," Robert said.

"I'm not," Tommy said. "I'm making it accurate."

A gull cried once, indignant at nothing. Far below, a wave found wood and retreated without apology.

"I am a husband," Robert said, because labels are often the last line men draw. "I am a father. I am a lector. I am the sort of lawyer people come to because I will not surprise them."

"Are you," Tommy said softly, "anything you need."

Robert breathed in. The air off the water had the faint metal of weather slowly changing its mind. "Need is a word we use when want frightens us."

"That's language," Tommy said. "It isn't an answer."

A couple passed behind them, talking low. The boy ran ahead, turned, ran back, his sneakers scuffing the boards, adding commas to a sentence the night was trying to speak.

"When did it start for you," Robert asked, voice barely more than the water. "This...whatever this is."

Tommy smiled without showing teeth. "Plant City," he said. "Seventeen. A long summer. Too much road and not enough shade. Then I spent ten years pretending it was a weather pattern and not a climate." He looked at Robert full. "You?"

Robert didn't glance away. "I've been walking with the map upside down for so long I forgot it could be read the other way."

They let that live in the air between them until it softened from confession to fact.

"I won't ask you to break anything," Tommy said. "I'm not the man who comes to take."

"You already did," Robert said, and surprised himself with how light the truth was when it finally landed. "You took away the lie that I was fine."

Tommy laughed once, low. "I'll pay for that," he said.

"Me too."

They didn't move. Proximity has its own grammar; theirs was careful, a language learned late. The hovering of a hand over the rail and not placing it. The way breath changes when the space between shoulders narrows. The tilt of the body that never quite becomes lean.

"You went to Hank's," Tommy said after a while, not a question, not a charge.

"I went to sit in a room where a man could be no one," Robert said. "I failed."

"That's because you are not no one," Tommy said. "Infuriatingly."

A freighter far off dragged a string of lights through the black, patient as a hymn. The line they made looked like handwriting against the horizon. Robert imagined copying it out until his wrist hurt and sliding the paper across a desk to someone who would know what it meant.

"I dreamt last night," he said. "We were driving a road east, out past the groves, and the radio was broken and we didn't mind. When I woke up, I could smell oranges."

"Plant City," Tommy said again, and for a moment his grin was the old one—easy, dangerous, beautiful.

"I do not want to hurt her," Robert said, the words coming raw. "That matters."

"I know," Tommy said. "It matters and it won't save anybody."

They let the sentence sit like a third man at the rail.

A gust came off the water and pushed their shirts against their backs, the kind of wind that isn't cold and still manages to feel like a warning. The couple turned back. The boy had gotten tired of running and was dragging his fingers along the slats, making a washboard music that set Robert's teeth on edge.

"I keep thinking there's an honorable version of this," Robert said. "If I say the right thing in the right room. If I time it like a gentleman. If I bleed in a straight line."

Tommy shook his head. "There isn't. There's only the version where you don't lie about what you're doing and you try to leave everyone with as much dignity as they can carry. It still hurts."

"Elaine will know," Robert said.

"She already does," Tommy said, not unkind. "That's how the good ones survive. They feel it a second before you say it and choose whether to help you be honest."

Robert closed his eyes long enough to see the parish hall under fluorescent light, the quilt, the raffle basket, the way Elaine's hand had found his after the reading and pressed exactly once. When he opened them, the bay looked closer.

"I won't kiss you tonight," Tommy said, a declaration and a comfort and a cruelty all at once. "I won't touch your sleeve. Not because I don't want to. Because once we cross that line, the rest will come like weather."

Robert's shoulders loosened a fraction—acceptance or defeat, he couldn't tell. He nodded. "Tomorrow," he said, surprising himself with the word he chose. It tasted like despair and relief.

"We've been saying tomorrow a long time," Tommy said. "All right. Tomorrow."

A siren burred far inland and quieted. The wind shifted. Someone somewhere dropped a bottle and the sound skipped along the boards and fell into the water. The boy yawned and leaned into the couple's legs and the couple turned home.

They walked back the length of the pier with more space between them than when they'd come, as if distance could keep intentions polite. In the lot, they paused between the dull pewter of Robert's hood and the dull red of Tommy's taillights.

"You'll be all right," Tommy said. "Not because this is easy. Because you are."

Robert wanted to ask for something—permission, absolution, directions—but all of it would have been cowardice dressed as need. He said, "Drive safe."

Tommy nodded. "You too."

They didn't shake hands. They didn't do anything theatrical or small. Tommy got in his car and watched the mirror for a beat too long before he turned onto 2nd. Robert started the Buick and let it idle until the sound of the engine measured his breath.

On 4th, a group of kids moved like loose electricity across the street, and he waited for them and remembered being that alive. At the light, he found his reflection in the window of a travel agency that advertised places with water the wrong color. He looked like a man making a mistake slowly and hoping slowness counted.

He arrived at the house the way decent men do—quietly, with keys in his palm so they wouldn't ring. Inside, he stood at the foot of the stairs long enough for the hallway to accept him. Elaine stirred when he entered the room and didn't wake. He sat on the edge of the bed and put his head in his hands the way men do when they are trying to pray without making God complicit.

He lay down and faced the window. The city pressed its dark face to the glass and waited to see who he'd be.

# 9

# GOSSIP AND OTHER FORECASTS

Morning came with the sound of cicadas—too many, too loud. The city was drying out, heat coming back in waves. Robert pressed his shirt collar flat and told the mirror the same lie he'd told every morning for months: *you look fine.*

At the office, the air smelled of paper and the faint sweetness of rain that had found its way into plaster. Margaret was already there, watering the plant that never died and never thrived.

"You look like you lost an argument with the weather," she said.

"I lost an argument with the night," he said before he could stop himself.

She gave him that small, knowing glance that women of her age and intelligence reserved for men like him—gentle pity wrapped in humor. "Then start winning the mornings again," she said, and went back to her watering.

Greer arrived half an hour later, on time and unshaven, humming the same tune the jukebox had coughed up at Hank's the week before. He greeted Margaret, nodded to

Robert, and went straight to his office. No words exchanged, but the air shifted—*something* unspoken but understood had taken a seat between their doors.

By mid-afternoon, the phones slowed. Rain threatened again but didn't follow through. Robert read the same line of a deposition three times before realizing it. Margaret leaned on his doorframe.

"You've both been ghosts lately," she said.

"Who?"

"You and Greer. The partners who think they're invisible. News for you—paperwork still shows up in daylight."

"We're fine."

"Fine," she repeated, as if the word were a loose tooth. "I've seen that look before."

"What look?"

"The one that says the story's already written, and you're pretending you're still editing."

She left before he could answer.

———

By the time he looked up again, the office had emptied. Through the blinds, the streetlamps were already burning amber. The sky was the gray-blue that only happens after storms have drained the city's patience.

He closed the file. His hand hesitated on the lock, then didn't bother. He drove without thinking—past the courthouse, past the bait shop, the same route his car seemed to know better than he did.

The motel sat near the edge of the marina—cheap, clean, anonymous. The sign's red vacancy flickered like a warning. He parked two spaces from a blue sedan he recognized. He didn't knock; the door opened before he reached it.

Tommy stood there, sleeves rolled, no tie, the kind of

man who looked like he'd stopped trying to disguise himself. The room smelled faintly of salt and coffee. One lamp burned low. The blinds were half-drawn.

"I didn't think you'd come," Tommy said.

"I didn't think I'd stay home," Robert said.

Tommy smiled. "That's progress."

Robert stepped inside. The air-conditioning hummed a cheap hymn. A single bed, a small table, a window that showed a slice of bay water between power lines.

"I didn't get this for—" Tommy began.

"I know," Robert said.

They sat—two chairs, one table. The coffee was burnt. The silence was worse. For a long moment, neither spoke. The hum of the unit became a third person in the room.

Tommy finally said, "It's a hell of a thing, isn't it? To live half your life certain you're one kind of man and then find out you're something else entirely."

Robert looked at his hands. "It's a hell of a thing to realize you've been half alive."

Tommy nodded. "There's truth in that."

He leaned back, eyes on the window. "You ever think about leaving?"

"Where?"

"Everywhere," Tommy said. "Just leaving."

Robert shook his head. "Running is for men who still think the road leads somewhere new."

Tommy laughed once, softly. "You and your sermons."

"They're all I have," Robert said.

The silence returned. Outside, a car started, moved, faded. The room felt too small for what they weren't saying.

"Tell me," Tommy said. "What happens next?"

"I don't know."

"You do."

"I can't."

"Then don't name it," Tommy said. "Just sit here and be honest."

Robert looked at him. The light from the window split Tommy's face—half shadow, half truth. It made him look younger, or maybe it just made Robert feel older.

"Honest," Robert said, "is that I want to be here. And that it's wrong. And that I'll do it again."

Tommy's jaw tightened. "Then we're both already guilty."

Robert nodded. "Maybe that's a kind of freedom."

They stayed like that, close enough to hear each other breathe, far enough to pretend it wasn't a choice. The air conditioner kicked off, leaving a heat that felt alive.

After a while, Tommy stood. "I can't ask you to stay."

"I can't ask you to stop," Robert said.

Tommy smiled, sad and sure. "Then we understand each other."

Robert stood, too. The distance between them wasn't much, but it was everything. He reached for the door.

"Tomorrow," Tommy said.

Robert stopped. "You always say that."

"I mean it every time."

Robert didn't turn. "So do I."

He opened the door. The night outside smelled of jasmine and motor oil. Somewhere across the bay, lightning flashed once, far and wordless.

He didn't look back.

———

Back at the office, the next morning came with new gossip. Danny was delivering pastries again, eyes bright with something unsaid. Margaret took her coffee black and her tone quieter.

"Whatever this is," she said, stopping at Robert's desk, "end it before it ends you."

He didn't ask how she knew. Some people don't need to see the fire to know the house is burning.

"Do me that favor," she said, softer now. "For the kids. For the decent part of you that still listens."

He nodded. "I'll try."

She studied him a moment longer. "Try faster."

She left him with his pen, his paper, and a conscience that wouldn't stop humming.

# 10

# WHILE THE LIGHTS ARE ON

August pressed down like a hand. The bay glittered in that particular cruel way—beautiful and not kind. In the parish office, the ceiling fans made their case without winning it. Elaine stood at the copier feeding pledge forms and thinking about numbers because numbers behave when you ask them to.

"Elaine?" said Ruth from the altar guild, too bright. "Do you have a moment?"

"Of course," Elaine said, turning with her smile in place —the one she wore for fundraisers and flu seasons.

Ruth approached as if she were holding a bowl of water to the brim. "It's probably nothing," she said. "It always is. I just thought... better from a friend."

"Better than what?" Elaine asked gently, already knowing the shape if not the name.

"Oh, you know how people are," Ruth said, eyes soft, voice soft, the sentence hard. "There's talk about Mr. Kelly spending too many evenings downtown. I said, 'Nonsense, Elaine's Robert is a lector,' but you know how talk is, it doesn't need proof to feel true."

Elaine's smile didn't shift. It didn't have to; she'd learned the trick long ago—keep the face, move the breath. "Well," she said, "summer makes people restless."

"Heat," Ruth said, grateful to be forgiven for delivering the package she'd brought. "Everything swells in this weather."

"Everything," Elaine agreed, and watched a number print neat and legible on paper.

After Ruth left, Elaine stood with her hand resting flat on the warm machine. She wasn't surprised. She recognized the feeling from years ago—rain changing direction without warning, wet where you didn't think to set a towel.

She finished the stack and stacked it again. She wrote a note for Father Donnelly about candles and left it in his box. She answered three questions that had nothing to do with her life and everything to do with the life of the church. Then she walked out into the noon glare and the city hit her with its usual mixture of noise and heat and the faint sweetness of something wilting.

At the light on 4th, she watched a group of teenagers cross slow, the dare in their bodies casual. A motel sign blinked. A diner door opened and closed and opened again. The day kept being the day. She drove home with the radio low, listening to the gentle, competent voice say high pressure, scattered showers, traffic on 22nd, the Cardinals at seven.

In the kitchen, she set the grocery bag on the counter and took each thing out carefully, as if silence might be reading the labels.

————

Robert came in early for once. He stood a second in the doorway like a man checking the weather from the porch. "You beat me," he said, quietly pleased and quietly wary.

"I had to be at the parish," she said, lining up cans—tomatoes, beans, tomatoes again. "Pledge form chaos."

He kissed her cheek. "You keep them together."

"I like order," she said. She turned to him, leaned back against the counter, and looked at his face as if it were the ledger she balanced every spring. "How was your day?"

"The same," he said. "Files, phones. Margaret threatened to demote me to courier."

"She could run that office," Elaine said. "She does."

He smiled. "She does."

She held his gaze one heartbeat past easy. "Were you downtown last night?"

He didn't blink, and the control cost him. "I drove," he said. "It helps me think."

"Does it?"

"Sometimes."

She nodded as if he'd told her about a tire that needed air. "We're having chicken," she said. "Will you set the table?"

"Of course."

He took plates from the cabinet, the ones with the thin blue ring, the wedding-gift set that had outlived three toasters. He placed them carefully, forks on the left, knives on the right, the way a decent man sets a table when he is trying to be decent. Elaine watched his hands and loved them and resented them and wanted nothing more than for them to remain exactly where they were.

The children tumbled in, bringing a breeze and a smell like sun. Anna asked if saints ever get mad and Elaine said of course, and Matthew said the word *throttle* three times because it felt good in his mouth. They ate, and family dinner did the trick it always does—it made an island.

Robert was good at islands. He asked the right questions. He cut the chicken for the smaller fork. He laughed at the correct moment and shook his head at the story that deserved a shake. He could have taught a course on ordinary.

During dishes, Elaine said, "I saw Ruth."

He dried a plate. "How is she?"

"Thirsty," Elaine said, and that got his attention.

He set the towel down. "What did she say."

"Oh, only that people are restless. Downtown. Evenings. That sort of weather-talk."

Robert looked at the sink. "People talk."

"They do," Elaine said. She passed him the last glass and turned off the water. "It must be strange," she added, mild as milk, "to be the subject of a weather report."

He dried the glass twice. "I drove," he said again, quieter.

She nodded. "I heard you."

They cleaned the table. He stacked the chairs slightly to vacuum the next morning. She folded the dishcloth. Domestic theater is not falsity; it's prayer in another language. But tonight the liturgy meant more, because the congregation needed convincing.

After, they sat in the small living room with their separate books. The fan sighed. The radio murmured about a tropical depression as if it were a guest you had to plan for. Elaine read three pages and could not have told you a word.

Robert turned a page with the carefulness of a man handling thin paper in a hot room. She watched the edge of the page lift, hesitate, settle. He would look good reading on a train, she thought. He would look good reading anywhere. It infuriated her.

"I'm meeting with the choir board on Thursday," she said.

"Will you win," he asked, reflexive tease.

"I always do."

He smiled, and the smile was the one from twenty years ago, a shape that had closed deals and opened doors and sealed vows. She hated that the memory made her chest feel both heavier and lighter.

"Robert," she said, setting the book on her lap. She did not change her voice. She did not raise it. She placed the sentence on the table between them like a folded letter. "Is there something you need to tell me."

He didn't look away. That was the only mercy he had left. "There is something I need to understand," he said finally. "Before I bring it here."

She breathed once—slow, steady. "I don't want the parish to tell me my life," she said. "I want you to."

"I know."

"When you're ready," she said.

"When I'm brave," he said, and flinched at his own accuracy.

She picked the book back up and did not open it. "Brave isn't what I married," she said. "Steady is. I'm finding out which one helps us more."

He nodded, a man agreeing to terms he hadn't known were on the page. They sat, and the room did that trick it does in old houses—the walls widened just enough to hold what didn't fit.

At nine-thirty, she stood, kissed his temple, and said, "Lock up?" the way she always said it. He touched her wrist as she passed, and she let him, and neither mentioned the heat in the small space that gesture made.

In bed, she lay on her side and looked at the window. The night pressed its face to the screen and listened. She closed her eyes and saw the parish hall, the raffle basket, the quilt, the way women tell each other things as if we were all one long, continuous conversation. She forgave Ruth. She forgave herself. She did not forgive the heat.

Beside her, Robert came in quietly. The mattress took him in the way it always did. She heard him breathe like a man who'd learned to make his body quiet. After a time, the sound evened, and she watched the ceiling go from gray to almost dark and back again. When she slept, it was the shallow sleep you bring home from hospitals.

———

In the morning, Elaine drove to the grocer on 9th early, when the air could still be called air. Near the doors, Danny Lee wrestled a crate of oranges onto a dolly, long limbs and earnestness and a face that wanted to be kind.

"Aunt Margaret says hello," he blurted when he saw her. He'd never learned how to move slowly through a greeting; it all arrived at once.

"Tell her hello back," Elaine said. "How are you, Danny?"

"Trying not to break anything," he said, gesturing at the fruit as if he were responsible for the entire citrus industry of Florida. Then, like a boy realizing he's stepped onto ice that might crack, he added, "The Kellys are good people."

"We are," Elaine said, and watched his relief arrive like a small dog begging to be let inside.

In the produce aisle, she took her time. She tested the peppers and rejected the ones that bruised under the thumb. A woman she knew from the Tuesday rosary asked whether extra volunteers were needed for the rummage sale; Elaine said always. A man from the choir said his wife had loved Robert's reading, "So steady—I told her it's what the parish needs." Elaine smiled and said thank you and pictured the word *steady* on a banner hung across their living room and let herself dislike it for the first time.

When she got home, she wiped the countertops as if the act could move heat out of the room. She set the oranges in a bowl on the table, each one bright and complicated. She pressed her thumb lightly into the skin of one and held it to her nose. Plant City, she thought. She didn't know why the name had come. She let it sit.

———

At the office, Margaret delivered gossip in the way decent people do—by not delivering it at all. She typed. She made calls. She brought Robert a file and a glass of water and put them down like facts. When he thanked her, she looked at him over her glasses.

"You have a good wife," she said. It wasn't a warning. It wasn't a benediction. It was the weather.

"I know," he said.

"Sometimes knowing's the last thing a man does before he forgets."

He nodded once. "I'm trying to remember."

"Try out loud," she said, and left him to the legal language that had always been good at saying the wrong thing the right way.

At lunch, the café's awning threw shade like a favor. Robert sat with a sandwich he didn't eat and watched the street behave. Tommy didn't appear. That was merciful. That was worse.

By late afternoon, the air felt like it had edges. The courthouse's hallways smelled of old air-conditioning and old arguments. Robert managed his hearings and his nods. The day ended because days do, not because anyone did the correct thing.

———

That evening, the house looked like a picture in a magazine from the 60s—lamp on, curtains curious, a woman at the sink not suffering and not sublime. Elaine plated dinner and the four of them ate and the conversation ran its rails. After, she stacked and rinsed and handed him the towel. He dried.

"You'll be late tomorrow?" she asked, as if checking the weather.

"Likely," he said.

She nodded as if the forecast had matched the map. "I'll keep the porch light on," she said, and made it sound like mercy when it was jurisdiction.

He kissed her cheek. "Thank you."

"Robert," she said, without turning. "If you have something to bring into this house, do it while the lights are on."

"I will," he said, and the lie felt like a dime under his tongue.

She turned then, and in her face lived the thing that would break him more than any shouting could—patience weaponized into grace. "I'm not going to ask again," she said, not unkind. "I'm going to wait. That's worse."

He nodded, almost bowed, and stood in the kitchen like a man who had been given a sentence and told to carry it in his pocket.

That night, when he left, he told himself he was only going for a drive. And he was. He drove past Hank's and didn't stop. He drove past the pier and did. He stood at the rail and thought about how water keeps secrets not out of kindness but because it doesn't know what else to do.

In the morning, Elaine laid out school clothes and packed lunches and wrote a check to St. Jude's and folded the dishcloth over the oven handle and waited for the part of the day when the house told her the truth. It did not arrive. That was its own truth.

She picked up the phone and dialed Margaret and didn't

complete the call. She set the receiver down and smoothed the edge of the table runner. Then she sat in the living room, hands in her lap, and gave the silence permission to speak.

It said only: *Soon.*

# 11

# TALLAHASSEE

S eptember slipped a notch cooler, the kind of change you only notice when the sun goes down and the air forgets to press. The bay kept its color. The city pretended time could be measured by school calendars and parish bulletins. In the office, Margaret flipped the page of the wall planner and said, "Well," like a woman speaking a eulogy for a month.

Tommy came in at nine with a folder tucked under his arm and an expression you wear to weddings and courtrooms. He set the folder on Robert's desk without sitting. "Tallahassee," he said, and the word already sounded like a place he'd been.

Robert stared at the folder's edge. "Policy job?"

"Something with a seal on the letterhead," Tommy said. "Enough daylight to call it respectable."

"When."

"End of the week."

Margaret appeared in the doorway with a pad and a pencil like a stage manager who has decided the play will make curtain whether the actors deserve it or not. She looked at the folder, then at the men, then at the calendar as if to confirm what the days already knew. "I'll draft the letter," she said. "You'll both sign. And you, Mr. Greer, will send me a forwarding address that is not a P.O. box."

Tommy smiled with half his face. "Yes, ma'am."

She clicked her pencil once. "Congratulations," she said, managing to make the word mean three other things. Then she left them with their furniture.

They didn't speak. Outside, a boy on a skateboard rattled down the block like an opinion. Somewhere in the building, a radio talked about traffic on 275 and a chance of showers.

"Why Tallahassee," Robert asked finally.

"It's away," Tommy said.

"From what."

"Don't make me catalog it," Tommy said, soft. "It won't help either of us."

Robert nodded. "You're right."

Tommy took a breath and set it down on the desk beside the folder. "Tonight," he said. "The pier."

"Of course," Robert said, and the certainty in his voice startled him.

———

Elaine made dinner that tasted like late summer—tomatoes, basil, the sweetness you only get when you eat them on time. The children told the day in a series of collisions and triumphs. Robert listened and picked up forks that fell and asked the questions fathers ask when they want to be men their children can trust.

After dishes, Elaine wiped the counter and handed him a towel and said, "You look like a man who owes the night something."

"I'll be back," he said.

"I know," she said.

He left the porch light on because she insisted, and because the square of glow on the walk had become a kind of mercy he didn't deserve.

He drove without the radio. The city at dusk looked like a confession written in pencil—erasures and pressure marks, truth smudged but visible. He passed the diner and Hank's and didn't slow. At the end of Central, the inverted pyramid made its usual impossible argument with the sky.

The parking lot held a handful of cars, none of which he recognized until one pair of headlights flashed once. He pulled in beside the blue sedan and shut off the engine. For a moment he sat with his hands on the wheel and tried to organize his breath into something that felt like endurance.

Tommy stood by the rail, sleeves rolled, no tie. The wind off the bay had found its autumn note—still warm, but carrying the first hint that the season might remember how to be kind. Robert walked the boards and they didn't speak until he reached him, because the distance needed to be honored.

"You look like Tallahassee already," Robert said.

"That's just sweat," Tommy said. "They make it there too."

They leaned on the rail with their shoulders not quite touching. The water below moved with purpose toward no destination anyone on land could name. A boy on a bicycle rolled past and lifted his front wheel an inch because it felt good to do a small, useless trick.

"Margaret said congratulations," Tommy said.

"She meant drive carefully," Robert said.

"She meant don't come back a smaller man," Tommy said. "She's better at the language than we are."

They watched a shrimp boat cross the mouth of the bay, its lights strung like a practical Christmas. Robert thought of the motel window and the hum of the air conditioner and the conversation that had made them both older. He thought of the parish hall and the quilt and Elaine's steady hand on a stack of plates. He thought of the word *tomorrow* and how it had done so much work and was now, inexplicably, unemployed.

"Say it," Tommy said, not looking at him.

"What."

"The thing you brought here to say."

Robert swallowed. The air tasted like salt and iron and the edge of rain. "You leaving doesn't save me," he said. "It just gives me one less place to put the truth."

Tommy nodded. "It saves me from watching you learn to tell it."

"That's not mercy," Robert said.

"It is for me," Tommy said, and finally turned. "I could stay. I could ask you to leave with me. I could make speeches about being brave. But we'd just be two men in a different city with the same weather."

Robert let the sentence sit; it fit poorly and exactly. "I won't beg you to stay."

"I didn't expect you to."

They stood quiet while the wind shifted and brought the smell of diesel and rope and someone frying something in a kitchen with the window open. The light on the end of the pier clicked on, and the boards went from gray to stage.

"I'll miss this," Tommy said, tipping his chin toward the dark water as if it were a person. "The bay. The stupid pyramid. The way the city lets you walk around feeling like a man who could start over if he timed it with the tide."

"You could," Robert said.

"So could you," Tommy said.

They both knew better.

A gull landed and considered them and then the water and then them again, as if deciding which creature was more likely to feed it out of pity. It chose the water and was wrong.

"Elaine knows," Tommy said. "Not everything. Enough."

"I know."

"Does she forgive you."

"She's decided not to decide," Robert said. "It's worse."

"It's kinder," Tommy said.

They let that be true for a while. The boy on the bicycle circled back and went past without looking, the way good boys are taught.

"Plant City will say I left for money," Tommy said, a grin in it. "I'll let them."

"Let them," Robert said.

The first drops arrived—indecisive, exploratory. The kind of rain that makes you think you imagined it. Out on the horizon, heat lightning stitched a loose seam and didn't bother with sound.

"I kept the lighter," Tommy said. "From the motel. I don't smoke. I don't know why I took it."

"So you'd have a thing to leave behind," Robert said.

Tommy laughed softly. "We're ridiculous."

"We are," Robert agreed, and loved him for it.

They didn't touch. They did something more dangerous: they remembered everything at once and stayed still anyway. A wave hit wood and the pier gave that small animal shift underfoot that says *you are standing on a body*.

"Goodbye," Tommy said, not theatrical and not small.

Robert felt the word land in his chest and slide into a

place he had saved for nothing. "Drive carefully," he said, because it was the only blessing he trusted himself to give.

Tommy nodded. "Tell Margaret I sent her flowers she'll refuse."

"She'll put the card in a drawer," Robert said. "She'll know where it is for twenty years."

They turned together and walked back, counting boards the way you count steps in a house you're leaving. In the lot, Tommy rested his hand on the roof of the blue sedan for a second like a man blessing a child who refuses to stand still. He looked at Robert once, then looked away—mercy again —and slid behind the wheel.

The engine coughed, then caught. The headlights made a brief cathedral of the pylons and then narrowed into the practical cones of men who have places to be. Robert stepped back without meaning to. Tommy lifted two fingers from the wheel—half a salute, half a surrender—and pulled out, the taillights making two red parentheses around a sentence Robert didn't have the nerve to finish.

Rain decided to mean it. It came soft, then steadier. Robert stood and let his jacket take it, no hurry to shelter. The blue sedan turned at 2nd and became part of the street's grammar, then a clause, then a comma, then nothing.

He didn't chase. He didn't move for longer than made sense. The gull came back and stood on one leg and pretended it wasn't watching him fail to do anything heroic.

When he finally walked to his car, the lot had emptied to a logic—four shapes in the rain, one of them his. He sat without starting the engine and put his palms on the wheel and felt the small tremor of a man who has been very brave in the least useful way.

Lightning stitched again without thunder. He looked at

the pyramid at the end of the road and thought of all the prayers that had nothing to do with God.

He turned the key. The Buick agreed to help. He drove home with the wipers keeping time. The porch light was on, as promised, a square of mercy on concrete. He stood in it a moment, soaking, not going in. The city held its breath.

## 12

## WHAT THE BAY KEEPS

Winter in St. Petersburg is a rumor. The air turns mild, the light whitens, and everyone pretends the change matters. Christmas had come and gone quietly. The parish put away its creche and kept the poinsettias too long. The Kellys' house stayed clean in that careful way where every surface means restraint.

Elaine woke early now. She liked the half-hour before the rest of the house joined her—just coffee and the sound of nothing. Robert came down when he heard the cup set on the counter, same as always. They spoke like two people running a well-managed company: efficient, polite, solvent. There were still touches—small, cautious, administratively tender. Some nights he'd feel her hand slide across his chest in sleep, searching for the old shape of trust, and he'd stay perfectly still so she could find it.

At work, Margaret kept her promise: no talk, no indulgence. She had turned the calendar again, new year at the top, the paper smelling of ink and opportunity. "The world keeps scheduling itself," she said, handing him a file. "That's something." He nodded. She looked at him a moment

longer. "He sent a card," she said, voice neutral. "Tallahassee. Says they have more sun and fewer lies."

"Good combination," Robert said.

"I didn't read between the lines," she said. "I stopped
doing that last year."

He smiled the way you do when someone tells you a
joke that's meant to save you.

That week he accepted a small case for a church charity
—property line dispute, nothing glamorous. He drove out to
the neighborhood one morning, bay light slanting through
palm fronds, and realized halfway there that he was
breathing differently. It startled him to notice: the heart still
tried to survive even when you gave it bad instructions.

———

On Sunday, Father Donnelly asked him to read again.
"Same passage," the priest said, smiling. "Corinthians likes
you."

"Or it's testing me," Robert said, and the priest laughed
and called him superstitious.

The church was fuller than usual. Lent close enough to
make people virtuous for an hour. The stained glass still
threw its good geometry on the pews. Elaine sat near the
aisle, hair pinned, children grown into quieter versions of
themselves. She looked up when he took the step to the
lectern, not with suspicion, not with pride, but with the kind
of patience that had learned its limits.

He began: "Love is patient, love is kind..." The words
found him again, but not as defense. He read them slowly,
carefully, as if each one were a small bridge and he had time
to test whether it would hold. His voice trembled once, only
once, on the word *endures*. He caught it, let it live, and kept
going.

When he finished, there was the brief hush before the

next hymn—every service's secret heartbeat—and he thought he could almost hear the bay beyond the walls.

————

After Mass, Elaine waited near the steps. "You sounded honest," she said.

"I tried."

"You almost believed it."

"I'm working on that."

She nodded. "We both are."

He drove alone for a while after. The sky was washed clean; the air had that faint citrus the city gets when the wind comes from inland. He didn't aim the car. It found the route. The pier had been repainted—new boards near the rail, a sign warning about high tides, the pyramid still pretending permanence.

He walked out as far as the second lamp, stopped where the wood changed shade, and leaned his hands on the rail. The water below had that slate-blue calm of early spring, small swells murmuring against pylons. For a moment he thought the surface looked familiar. Then he saw it: a glint, small, caught between boards.

He crouched. The object was nothing special—a lighter, scratched, cheap, one of those motel kinds. He turned it over once. On the back, faint letters carved with a key: *T*.

He smiled, but not the kind you see. He set it in his palm, the metal warm from the sun. For a long minute, he stood there, thumb on the wheel, not flicking it, just feeling the weight of something that refused to vanish. The wind picked up, and the lighter gave off the faint smell of fuel, like the memory of a flame.

He didn't put it in his pocket. He left it on the rail. He leaned beside it, both of them facing the water.

The bay held its breath, the pyramid's reflection steady

and upside-down, heaven inverted but still bright. A pelican cut a slow arc above the channel. Somewhere behind him a child laughed, sharp and clean, and the sound landed like forgiveness.

Robert whispered, almost to the water, "All right."

He didn't mean all right as in fine. He meant it as in *I'll stay alive.*

He turned toward the parking lot, slower now. The sky behind the city had begun to pink at the edges. He thought, not for the first time, that hope was just the moment before light touches the water and decides to stay.